'I'm going to 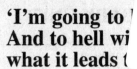 And to hell with what it leads t

So he kissed her, and she loved it. But after a while it was he who broke it off. He eased her from him, held her at arm's length and said, 'We've got some kind of precarious balance between us. We're close, but not too close. And this is rocking the balance.'

'You can't balance for the rest of your life. You're going to have to come down on one side or the other.'

'I've balanced it so far,' he said. 'Tell me, though, what d'you think my choices are? What sides do I have to choose between?'

'Me or not me,' she said. 'And, Harry, the choice is yours.'

SPECIAL CARE BABY UNIT

**Special babies, special carers—
lives lived moment to moment . . .
heartbeat to heartbeat**

Dear Reader

My daughter Helen trained as a midwife, but now works mostly in a SCBU. I have seen her feeding a baby so small that she could hold it in one hand. It's work that she loves. It's hard, but so often rewarding.

SCBU work is intensive. The staff—doctors, nurses, ancillary workers—are thrown together in an intimate and often intense working environment. This intimacy often affects their personal lives. It is that very intimacy, and the level of care that I saw being administered to those tiny babies, that influenced me to write this series of stories.

Each of the three stories features a dedicated heroine who discovers that you need more than work to be completely fulfilled.

I hope that you enjoy reading them.

With best wishes,

Gill Sanderson

EMERGENCY: BACHELOR DOCTOR

BY

GILL SANDERSON

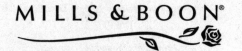

MILLS & BOON®

TO ELSIE, VICKY AND ROBBIE—
LONG-TIME FRIENDS

*First published in Great Britain 2004
Harlequin Mills & Boon Limited,
Eton House, 18-24 Paradise Road, Richmond, Surrey TW9 1SR*

© Gill Sanderson 2004

ISBN 0 263 83916 8

*Set in Times Roman 10½ on 12 pt.
03-0804-46159*

*Printed and bound in Spain
by Litografia Rosés, S.A., Barcelona*

CHAPTER ONE

'YOU'VE done well, Bessie,' one-year-qualified Dr Kim Hunter murmured. 'You've done very well. I've done my absolute best to look after you and I'm pleased with what you've managed today. Now, just one last five-minute effort.'

She guessed that the temperature should be down by now, so she slapped Bessie's red side and the old car shook slightly. Her engine gave three or four of the ominous ticks that had become more and more common recently, but when Kim climbed back in she started willingly enough.

Now that Kim was a senior house officer her pay would go up—slightly. Perhaps she should think about a new car. A more dignified car that suited a professional person such as she was—or would be soon. A person starting a new life. Bessie had been with her for five years, it was time she was pensioned off. Kim had promised her to the young lad who lived next door to her parents.

'Soon I'll give you to Mickey,' Kim said, 'he'll love you, and give you all the tender loving care that you need.'

Tender loving care, Kim thought, and grinned sourly to herself. What a wonderful phrase! And there were words like trust, and fidelity, and loyalty and commitment. Then she reminded herself that she had decided that the best way to deal with the foun-

5

dering of her relationship with Robin Webb was to
treat it as the rather bad joke that it was. Now she
was free! And she knew that, after the initial shock,
it felt good. Parting from Robin had been a good
thing.

'I care for nobody, no, not I,' Kim sang loudly as
Bessie slowly ascended the last hill, 'and nobody
cares for me.'

Not exactly true, of course. She cared for her parents, her family, the large number of friends she was
leaving behind. But not for Robin any more. Now
she would happily forget him and their half comic,
half tragic parting. This was the start of a new, man-
free life. She was here for six months. She'd do nothing but work.

Bessie made the top of the hill and Kim pulled in
to look at the view. It was good British landscape at
its best. Below her was the little seaside town of
Denham and beyond it the blue, sparkling sea. She
could see the harbour, the long beaches to one side
of the town, the white cliffs to the other. And just
below her was the Wolds Hospital. She could see its
lawns, the buildings, often hidden by trees. A stark
contrast to the city-centre hospital she had just left.

It was August, almost exactly a year since Kim
had qualified as a doctor. Since then she had per-
formed two six-month periods as a house officer in
her old hospital—one in a medical ward, the other in
a surgical ward. Now she was a senior house officer
and intended to do two more six-month periods on
rotation. First she was here, to work in the paediatric
department. For her second period she would probably go back to Sheffield and work in A and E. And

then she could start on her chosen career. She would train to be a GP.

'Time to get started, Bessie,' Kim said, and the old car slowly dropped down the hill.

Kim knew her way around the hospital, she'd had a thorough introduction when she'd come here for her interview. She picked up her keys from Security, drove straight to the doctors' residence where she had been allocated a tiny flat. It took her a while to carry up the cases, cardboard boxes and bags that held all that she might need for the next six months.

She could have left some stuff behind. But after arguing so completely—and so satisfyingly—with Robin, it hadn't seemed fair to try to store her goods with him. Even though half the equity in the flat was still technically hers.

It took her a couple of hours to unpack, to make the place look a little like home. Then she took off her T-shirt and jeans, showered and opened her wardrobe. What to wear? It was important to make the right first impression. And Kim knew that too often she looked un-doctor-like.

It had been cooler when she'd come for her first interview and she had worn the traditional dark suit recommended to all doctors, male or female. But now it was hot, not at all suit weather. Some kind of dress perhaps.

She was only half an inch under six feet tall. Her shoulders were, well, broadish. She wore her dark hair very long, almost to her waist. It was impractical, of course, but when she was on the wards it was only the work of five minutes to put it up in a pleat.

Still, she didn't present the usual picture of a female doctor.

In the past some patients had seen her size as almost a challenge. Well, that was their hard luck.

Eventually she decided on a light blue cotton dress, of a reasonable length and with not too much cleavage showing. Too hot for tights, but a sensible pair of strappy white sandals. A touch of make-up and her hair loose but held back by two combs. Yes, quite a doctor-like ensemble. As much of one as she could manage in this heat.

She was due to report in tomorrow morning, not to her ward but for the induction process that all staff had to go through. This, she knew, was a good idea. Different hospitals had different ways of doing things. But that was tomorrow. There was no reason why she shouldn't go to the paediatric department, introduce herself and get a bit of a feel of the place.

She got her first shock when she arrived at the receptionists' desk. She wasn't expected—not only tomorrow, but not at all.

The flustered secretary leafed through papers on her desk, opened drawers and searched her in-tray. Then she smiled proudly, having found the necessary bit of paper. 'Yes, there's been a bit of a change, Dr Hunter, just for a while. You're not to start here but in SCBU. That's the special care baby unit.'

Kim blinked. This was a bit of a shock.

'You will have it all explained on your induction course. Would you like me to find a senior member of staff to talk to you now?'

SCBU. Dealing with premature babies, those needing extra-special care. Kim had almost no experience of that kind of work, though, as she thought about it, it appealed to her. She'd learn a lot. 'Don't worry,' she said with a smile. 'It's my fault for turning up early. I'll just walk over to SCBU and say hello. Thanks for your help.'

But she frowned as she walked over to the special unit. The work might be interesting, but when she was a GP she wouldn't see many babies needing this kind of attention. Most GPs dealt only with normal births. Still…it might only be for a month or so.

She reported to the SCBU receptionist, who said that she was in luck. Chris Fielding, the consultant, was in and would love to see her. A nurse came and escorted her through the locked door, past the equipment store, the laundry, the linen store, past the parents' sitting room and then the four nurseries. She caught glimpses of the babies, so tiny in their transparent incubators. And then she was taken into the doctors' room and introduced to Chris Fielding.

She'd met him briefly before, when she'd come for interview. But, then, she'd met so many people those two days. Still, she remembered Chris. A tall, good-looking man. Hadn't she heard that he was engaged to one of the nurses in the department? He rose to shake her hand.

'Dr Hunter, I'm so glad to meet you. Now, let's get some coffee and then we'll have a bit of a chat. I think you're due an explanation and perhaps an apology. It must be a shock ending up here instead of in paediatrics, as you were expecting.'

She liked him at once. 'Not at all. I'm looking forward to learning from you.'

'Good. I have to explain that I fought to get you.

There are three SHOs coming to the paediatric section and I need one of them. When I saw your references, I thought you were the one I'd like to have.'

'It's always nice to be flattered,' she said cheerfully.

He grinned. 'No one gets flattered here. Any praise you get, you have to work hard for. Now, you know that there are no house officers in SCBU? The bottom rank of doctor is yours—senior house officer. And so it follows that you get to do all the dogsbody work. All the boring routine paperwork, the simplest of tests. You don't get much rest and you don't get much sleep.'

'I can cope with that.'

'I'm sure you can. But I won't have anyone in my department who doesn't get the chance to learn. At first you'll just watch. But we want to teach you. When you leave us I want you to have skills that will be of future use to you and to your patients. I'll discuss your programme with you later.'

'I'd like that,' Kim said. She was thinking that this was very different from the casual, dropped-in-at-the-deep-end approach that she'd met before. She would learn here.

'For the first couple of weeks you can—'

There was a knock at the door, a nurse opened it and peered at them. 'Chris…er, sorry, Mr Fielding, sorry to interrupt but I'm not very happy about baby North's breathing. When you're ready, if you've got a minute…'

'I'll come now, Eileen.'

Chris looked at Kim in her smart dress. 'I'd invite you to come along, Dr Hunter, but babies have a habit of being a bit messy.' He waved at a table, where she saw a coffee percolator and mugs. 'Why don't you help yourself to the coffee I offered you? I should be back in a couple of minutes.'

'Thank you,' said Kim. 'But, please, don't hurry for me.'

She thought she was going to like it here. She stood, poured herself a mug full of coffee, then bent to look at a photograph pinned to a cork board on the wall. A beaming, arm-waving baby. On the bottom of the photograph someone had written, 'Our baby, Charles Edward Lucas, now six months old. When he came into SCBU he was so tiny we didn't think he'd live. Your care pulled him round. Thanks to all the staff.'

That's nice, Kim thought. It was good to see actual proof of a success.

Perhaps it was her fault. The cork board was on the hinge side of the door, perhaps she should have expected that the door would swing open. But, then, she didn't expect that someone would push it open with so much vigour.

Whatever. Suddenly a loud male voice shouted, 'Congratulate me, Chris! I got the place.' The door swung open, propelled by fist or foot. And as it swung back it hit Kim's arm, causing her to drop the coffee-mug and spill coffee all the way down her front.

The mug bounced on the floor and she looked down in horror. There was a dark brown stain on her dress, all the way from neck to hemline.

A moment's stricken silence. And the voice said,

'Coming in like that wasn't the most intelligent thing I ever did, was it?'

'No,' Kim snapped. 'Quite frankly, it was the action of an idiot. I was trying to make a good impression here and now I look like a refugee from a works canteen.'

'We can find you a basin and you can put it in to soak, or whatever it is that ladies do,' the voice said. 'And I'm sure there'll be some scrubs that you can borrow.'

Vaguely, Kim registered that it was quite a pleasant voice. Deep and musical. And it sounded as if the speaker wasn't too worried about what he had done. In fact, he apparently found it rather amusing. Well, she wasn't amused!

She looked up at the newcomer, intending to fix him with a basilisk-like stare and tell him exactly what she thought of his behaviour. But suddenly things weren't the same any more. Why now, why this man, she didn't know. She just knew that things would never be the same again now she'd met him. A shiver ran down her back, the palms of her hands felt damp, she could feel her heart beating far faster than was normal or good. Who could he be?

He was tall, taller than she was. That was a good thing. Like her, he was broad-shouldered and now he stood like an athlete, poised as if ready to run, hit or throw. As she watched she saw him relax, his body seeming to become less taut. He looked at ease with himself.

He had been dressed in a smart dark lightweight suit, but the jacket was now thrown over his shoulder, held by one finger. The blue silk tie had been loosened and flopped casually over the purest of white cotton shirts. Well, it was warm.

What was it about him?

He was smiling, and by the lines round his eyes it seemed that smiling was normal for him. None of his features was extra-remarkable, what made his face exciting was the life in it. His lips were quirked, as if he thought that life was a comedy. And then he looked at her directly and she saw his eyes. They were grey—no, not grey, they were silver. And if his mouth suggested that life was a joke, then the haunted depths of his eyes hinted that at times the joke wasn't very funny.

She pulled herself back to awareness, realising that for the past few moments she had been staring at him silently, like a love-sick teenager. Which she certainly wasn't. But, then, he had been silent, too. She felt—she knew—that he had felt the same shock of recognition as she had.

'This is a new dress,' she said, trying to recover. 'I would like to sponge it or something. And if there are any scrubs…?'

She saw him make an effort to recover himself. 'Come with me. When I explain to a nurse that I threw coffee all over you, she'll look at me with that pitying expression that I know so well. And she'll look after you because all the ladies here band together to cope with my daily disasters. We're a friendly team here.'

He led her to the nurses' room. A pretty nurse looked up as they entered and smiled. The man said, 'This is Nurse Erica Thornby. Erica, this young lady and I have just had a collision which was entirely my fault and she would like to rinse out her dress. Are there any scrubs she could borrow?'

Then he looked at Kim. 'You know, I don't know your name.'

'I'm Kim Hunter,' Kim said. 'I'm to be the SHO here for six months. Who're you?'

'Harry Black, bachelor of this parish. In fact, Dr Harry Black. I've been Specialist Registrar here for the past two years. But only for a few more months. Like you, I shall then leave.'

'Harry, you haven't got the job! We want you here.'

Kim saw that Erica, the nurse she'd just been introduced to, seemed quite concerned. Evidently Harry was a popular man.

'But I am also wanted in Australia. And in six months' time, while you are suffering the particular evils of a Denham winter, I shall be sunning myself on an Antipodean beach.'

'Look out for sharks and sunstroke,' Erica said. Then she turned to Kim, held out her hand. 'Hi, I'm Erica Thornby, staff nurse here so we'll be seeing a lot of each other. I'll find you some scrubs from the store and then we can put your dress to soak in the sluice.'

'That would be nice,' said Kim. Things seemed to be moving too fast for her, she felt she needed time to grasp what was happening. Chris Fielding, Harry Black, Erica Thornby, they were all making an impression. She wanted to work with them. Then she thought for a moment. Did she really want to work with Harry Black? It might be difficult.

Ten minutes later, now clad in green scrubs, she

was chatting to Erica in the sluice when Chris Fielding looked in.

'I gather from his profuse apologies that you've met Harry,' he said. 'In fact, you'll be spending a lot of time with him. I'll want you to shadow him for a few days. But for now… I know you haven't officially started yet, but we've got a bit of a problem and I thought you might like to watch. It's something I've got to deal with at once so we'll have to postpone our talk, I'm afraid. We've got a baby with IVH, I'm going to try to lower the pressure in her brain. Of course, you might have other plans so this is just a casual offer, if you're interested.'

'I am interested and I would like to watch,' said Kim. 'As I said, I'm here to learn.'

'Then we'll go and scrub up. Erica will find you gloves and a gown.'

They soaped and washed their hands and Chris asked, 'What do you know of IVH-intraventricular haemorrhage?'

'Not too much. I've heard of it but I've never seen a case. Isn't it when prem babies bleed into cavities in the brain?'

'That's more or less it. Often it's not dangerous and the condition clears itself up. But this baby has a build-up of fluid and we have to get rid of some of it. We've tried medication but that didn't work. Now we're going to perform a lumbar puncture.'

'Right,' said Kim.

When they were sufficiently sterile, Chris and Kim walked into the tiny ward. A gowned nurse had put the baby into the foetal position, holding him gently but firmly. Kim had assisted with lumbar punctures before, but only with adults. Sticking a needle into this tiny being must be a very delicate operation!

The baby's back was swabbed and sterilised. 'Point to where you think the needle should go,' Chris said.

Kim pointed, and Chris nodded his approval. 'Good. Now, let's draw off some of that fluid.'

Kim noticed that Chris used a very fine needle, sliding it carefully between the vertebrae. But unlike the usual lumbar puncture, there was no means of sucking out the fluid. Instead, Chris let the fluid drip out of the needle into a little vial. 'The last thing we need is to take too much,' he explained to her. 'This is a very tiny body. We need just sufficient to release the pressure. And I think that should be it.'

Kim found that unconsciously she had tensed and she sighed with relief when Chris eased out the needle.

'I found that a bit scary,' she said. 'I've no problem with the usual lumbar puncture but the baby seems so...small. Is that a foolish thing to say?'

'Not at all. A lot of people think that because our prems are so small, they are too tiny to cope with. They think nothing can be done for them. Parents are often afraid because they've produced someone so apparently helpless. But many thirty-week babies have as strong an urge to live as full-term babies. And it's a great job, helping them.' Chris smiled. 'I love the work and I'll bet in time you will.'

She looked at Chris. 'I'm fascinated but I'm also a bit nervous. D'you really want someone with as little experience as me? Aren't you afraid I might make a mistake?'

He shook his head. 'Not at all. If you're cautious, if you're always ready to ask for advice, you'll be fine. Now, how about that coffee I promised you? I gather you didn't manage to drink much of the first one.'

'I'll hold onto this one with both hands,' she told him.

He took her to the doctors' room again and poured her a coffee. He told her that they were an informal department and among themselves they always used first names. 'There'll be some times when I'll address you as Dr Hunter and you'll call me Mr Fielding. But I'm sure you'll recognise when it's necessary. Now, I'll tell you about the staff, and then you can meet them one by one. Something I want to emphasise. We're not doctors and nurses and ancillary workers here. We're all part of a team, and everyone's contribution is valuable. In the next few months you'll probably learn as much from the nurses here as you will from the doctors.'

'He's only saying that because he's going to marry one of the nurses,' a voice said. 'He's going to marry Jane Wilson, the ward manager here, and he's a very lucky man.'

Kim recognised the voice at once and she felt her breath catch in her throat. Harry Black. She looked up to see him cautiously opening the door and peering round it.

'The last time I opened this door,' Harry said, 'there was a woman waiting behind it, a dangerous cup of coffee in her hand. I'll be more careful in future.'

Chris smiled at Kim. 'I asked Harry to drop in,'

he said. 'Not only can he apologise again but we can talk about your future programme.'

Harry walked over to her, amiable, apparently relaxed, and offered his hand. 'Sorry about the dress,' he said. 'As a sign of penitence, would you like me to take it to the dry-cleaner's?'

'No need. The stain will wash out.' She thought back to when they had first met. 'And I'm sorry for calling you an idiot. Sometimes I speak before I think. It was just an accident. But can I ask you why you wanted to be congratulated?'

She saw Chris shaking his head, a reluctant smile on his face. 'I know it'll be good for your career, Harry,' he said. 'But we're going to miss you here. You're a hands-on doctor, not a pure scientist.'

'For a while I can be both. And if I get the Ph.D I'm working for, well, when I get back you'll have to call me doctor doctor.'

He turned to Kim. 'I've been offered a place in an Australian laboratory as part of a team doing biomedical research into mother-to-baby transfer through the placenta. We want to know what gets through, and how and why. And one or two days a week I shall work at the attached hospital as a neonatal doctor. It's supposed to be an attempt to bring pure science and practical medicine together.'

'And you'll be away for three years?' Chris asked.

'That's the time allowed for the Ph.D. But if they then offer me a job I couldn't resist, well…'

'Like I said, I'll miss you. Who else can I play squash with? In fact, the whole department will miss you.'

Kim realised that the two other people she had so

far met in the department had both said that Harry
would be missed. Evidently he was popular. She
could understand why.

Chris turned back to Kim. 'You've got the induction programme for the next two days. A lot of it
will be boring but it's all necessary. Then I'd like to
see you here on Wednesday morning—half past eight
be all right?'

'No trouble at all. I'm in the doctors' accommodation, it's a five-minute walk.'

'Good. I've asked Harry to show you round on
Wednesday morning. Tell you the kind of things that
we do, the work we'll want you to do. And you'll
also meet Jane Wilson, she's ward manager here…'

'Jane Wilson, soon to be Jane Fielding,' Harry
pointed out, and Kim saw Chris blush slightly.

'Harry, you make this place sound like a dating
agency! People come here to work, not to find part-
ners.'

'Work may be their intention but they do find part-
ners. Look at you all! You and Jane, Dominic Tate
and Petra Morgan, Erica Thornby and Matt Kershaw.
All in the past few months. I'm the only single man
who nobody wants.'

'It hasn't stopped you looking,' Chris said drily,
and Kim tried not to smile.

She was enjoying herself here. There was an atmosphere, a camaraderie, that she hadn't found in her
previous two placements. And yet she sensed that
under the good-natured joking there was a consid-
erable amount of professional pride. This was a
happy but efficient unit.

'Anyway,' Chris went on, 'Jane is the ward manager but she's very much involved with the practical work of the unit. Ask her anything, she knows as much about the work here as anyone. For the rest of the week, shadow Harry. And early next week we'll start you working on your own.'

He pushed a sheet of paper across to her. 'Look through this. It's an account of the duties you'll have to perform. If there's anything—'

The door was opened again, and this time Erica looked in. 'Baby Evans has spiked twice now,' she said. 'I'm a bit concerned.'

'I'll come to have a look,' Chris said. 'Harry, do you want to come as well? Kim, good to meet you and I'll see you Wednesday.' He held out his hand.

'Thanks for seeing me,' Kim said. 'I'm really looking forward to working here.'

'Under my expert tuition,' said Harry, also shaking her hand. 'Just before you go, Kim, I know the number of the doctors' flats, but what's your extension number?'

'Two six three,' said Kim.

'Easy to remember.' And Chris and Harry were gone.

Kim left the unit and walked across the lawns to her flat.

She stripped off her borrowed scrubs, pulled on shorts and a T-shirt. Then she made herself a mug of tea and reached for a packet of digestive biscuits. The only food she had brought with her had been tea, coffee and the biscuits she loved. When hours got longer and longer, in order to keep going other doctors ate chocolate. But for Kim the snack of choice had always been digestive biscuits.

She stretched out on her single easy chair, rested her feet on the coffee-table. After she'd finished the second biscuit, she realised that she was ravenous. She hadn't eaten since her early morning porridge. Soon she'd have to make a visit to a local supermarket or find her way to the hospital canteen—if it was still open.

She considered. It was only five o'clock but she seemed to have had a full day. She had driven—or coaxed—Bessie here from Sheffield. She had unpacked, visited her new unit, met some of the people she was going to work with. After her initial dismay she found she was rather looking forward to working in SCBU. And working with Chris and Harry.

She knew she was avoiding thinking about it, but it had to be done. What had she felt when she'd seen—and heard—Harry for the first time? Why had there been that electric moment? What had passed between them?

She felt slightly irritated. She was supposed to be a doctor, looking for scientific explanations. To be so suddenly and inexplicably attracted to a man was just not reasonable. And only a couple of hours after she had been congratulating herself on releasing herself from Robin, looking forward to a time free from tiring emotional entanglements. Of course, she was young and healthy, and had the usual hormonal reactions to attractive members of the opposite sex. Her feelings were quite natural, everyone had them.

But why had her reaction been so strong?

She felt more irritated than ever. So she'd been attracted to a man. It didn't mean she'd have to do anything about it. She'd keep Harry Black out of her life.

And the other thing was, she was sure that he had felt the same way. Harry was as attracted to her as she was attracted to him. There had been a spark in his eye—of surprise as much as anything.

She wondered why Harry had asked for her telephone number. She wondered when he would phone her. Where would they go from here?

She was just about to walk down into town when her phone rang. As it rang she looked at it suspiciously—was it going to get her into something she wasn't quite sure about? Should she just ignore it, walk on as she had intended? As far as she knew, there was only one person who knew her new phone number—and that was Harry. And she wasn't yet sure what she thought about him.

But then she answered. She'd never backed away from a fight and this had to be done.

'Kim? It's Harry Black here.'

Even though she was expecting it, the sound of his voice sent a thrill through her. There was an undercurrent of humour to it, as if they shared the deep secret that the world was really rather a strange place.

'Surprise me,' she said. 'So far you're the only person who has my phone number. What can I do for you, Harry?'

'You can have dinner with me. No, let's be more exact. You can let me buy you dinner. Consider it a further apology for ruining your dress.'

'My dress isn't ruined and you've apologised enough already. Do you invite all the SHOs out to dinner the day they arrive?'

'Only the extremely attractive ones,' he said blandly.

'I'll bet you say that to all the girls.' She thought for a moment. Was it a good idea to go out with this man on her very first day? Then she decided. She was tough, resilient, she could cope with the Harrys of this world and would have to cope with herself. If there was a problem, she'd get it out into the open.

'All right, I'll have dinner with you, Harry,' she said. 'But let's get one thing straight. I'm not a sweet, innocent little medical student, overwhelmed because a real live registrar is taking me out.'

'I'll bet you say that to all the boys. Now, there's a very pleasant pub called the Escott Arms, just a few yards away from the hospital entrance. A lot of the staff eat there. How about if I pick you up about seven and we'll walk over there?'

'I'll meet you inside, Harry,' she said. 'I'll find it. Bye.' Then she rang off. She didn't want him calling for her. Not until she was sure of how they would treat each other.

CHAPTER TWO

AN HOUR and a half before she was due to meet him. Plenty of time. She could work for an hour. So Kim dragged out her medical textbooks and her carefully filed notes and started to read up about premature babies. She knew something, of course, but a medical student never had time to learn everything. So she checked through what she knew. And what she didn't know.

She read about anaemia, hyaline membrane disease, broncho-pulmonary displasia, necrotising enterocolitis. It seemed hard that a tiny premature baby should have to fight off illnesses as well as cope with the problems caused by being born too early. But as she read she realised just how much had been learned about pre-term illnesses in the past thirty years. A lot of good work had been done. When she finished reading she was more interested than ever in her new department.

Time to change and go out. This was the second time today she'd had to make a decision about what to wear, but this time she wasn't going to agonise over it. She had a pretty white dress, shot with blue and silver, an ideal warm-weather dress. It would be ideal, smart enough for a dinner, casual enough to indicate that she wasn't over-eager. A quick ten minutes spent brushing hair and putting on make-up and then she was ready to find this Escott Arms. She was half apprehensive, half looking forward to the evening.

She found the place at once, an attractive-looking building with large numbers of people sitting outside on benches. And one of them rose as she appeared—Harry Black.

That odd little jerk somewhere in her midriff—she just wasn't used to reacting so quickly to a man, it had never happened before. She wasn't even sure that she liked it—but she certainly couldn't help it. What was it about Harry? If she was going to react this way every time she met him, she'd have to be extra-careful.

He, too, had changed and was now in blue linen trousers and a darker blue polo shirt. The two blues contrasted with the silver grey of his eyes. He smiled, held out both his hands to her.

'Good to see you, Kim. Welcome to the Escott Arms—it's almost an extension of the hospital.'

As she glanced round she knew this to be true. More than a few people were looking towards them, whilst pretending to look somewhere else. She might not be known—but Harry certainly was.

'It seems to be very pleasant,' she said. 'Is the food as good as the surroundings?'

'Probably even better. Do I take it from that question that you're hungry?'

'All I've had so far today is porridge and digestive biscuits. I'm ravenous.'

'Then let's go inside and order. I like a girl with an appetite.'

She looked at him sardonically. 'Down, Rover,' she said, and he laughed.

They were shown to a banquette—she was pleased to feel that there was air-conditioning inside. Both ordered quickly and then the waiter asked if they'd like anything to drink. Kim said, 'You can buy me dinner, but I'm buying the wine—and that decision isn't open to negotiation.'

'As you wish. I'm a red-wine man myself, but I'll drink anything. You're going to order?'

'I'll order and red wine it shall be.' She scanned the list the waiter put in her hand. 'There's a reasonable Rioja here.' She was glad he hadn't tried to argue, she'd met too many macho men who felt that their masculinity was being attacked if they couldn't order the wine.

They ordered, but would have to wait a while. Now it was time to talk, and she wondered what he would say. They were to be colleagues but she knew that this meeting was not about work.

She decided to be direct. 'Just to get things clear,' she said. 'I'm sitting here having dinner with you and I suspect that half the hospital will know about it tomorrow. I take it that you're not married or engaged or anything like that?'

He laughed, apparently not at all upset by her bluntness. 'I'm not married or anything like that. Not even in any temporary relationship. I'm feckless and fancy-free.'

'I can believe that,' she muttered, and then went on, 'Why aren't you married or anything like that? You're reasonably attractive and you apparently like women.'

This time he blinked. Then he said, 'Perhaps I like women, not one particular woman.'

'Oh, no,' she groaned, 'don't say I'm having dinner with Denham's answer to Don Juan. I hate men who think it's their duty to please as many women as possible.'

His answer was mild. 'Pleasing people is not something to be ashamed of. Let's just say that there are women I've been close to—and I think I'm still friendly with all of them.'

'That is an achievement. But no particular one at the moment?'

'No particular one. Life on the unit recently has been…hectic. And I've just taken part two of the Royal College exam. Working for that was hard work.'

Kim shivered. 'I finished all my exams last year. And after that I vowed never to take another paper again. I don't mind the hard work and I don't mind the studying. I just don't like sitting down in front of a piece of paper for three hours.'

'I agree. So your ambition is…?'

'I'm going to be a GP. My dad's a GP, it's all I've ever wanted. I'm going to work with him.'

He didn't speak for a moment. When he did his voice seemed different, a little harsher. 'You get on well with your parents?'

She looked at him in surprise. 'What kind of question is that? Of course I do.'

He didn't reply.

At that moment a smiling waitress appeared and put down their starters. A crab salad for her, grilled goat's cheese salad for him. They both looked fantastic.

She picked up her knife and fork. 'Enough talk about work and ambitions,' she said. 'Let's eat.'

'Let's eat,' he agreed.

The food was as good as it looked. But when their plates had been cleared away and a glass of wine poured for each of them, he said, 'Being a GP is a good ambition. But have you thought of being a hospital doctor? You might really like one of the specialities—working in SCBU, for example.'

She shook her head. 'My ex-partner…that is, someone I worked with…was always on at me to give up the idea of being a GP. He wanted me to join him in geriatrics. Said there was a great future in it.'

'It's certainly going to be a growth area. Whether there's as much satisfaction in it as paediatrics, I don't know. I've got a couple of friends who love the work. However, tell me more about this expartner.'

'Why d'you want to know?'

He beamed at her. 'Call it intellectual curiosity. But really it's just me being nosy. I find I have a deep interest in the welfare of those who work with me. Especially when they're gorgeous like you.'

'Well, that's very flattering. I ask myself if it's honest as well.'

She wondered if she should reveal herself so fully to this man. She hardly knew him, had met him less than eight hours ago. And she knew—she had been told—that she tended to take chances, to make decisions too quickly and on too flimsy grounds. Why should she confide in him? But she liked Harry and felt that she could trust him. He seemed sympathetic. She'd risk it.

'His name is Robin Webb, he's quite a bit older than me. Like you, he's a registrar and we've been— we were—living together for three years. Robin looks like a Greek god—you know, all golden curls, perfect profile and a beautiful brown tanned body.' She giggled. 'I only found out later that the tanned look took him hours in the gym tanning room and when he hadn't time in the gym he used to go to this beauty parlour that coated him in fake tan.'

'Sounds entrancing.' Harry's voice was dry. 'How could you bear to separate yourself from such a creature?'

Kim picked up the salt cellar and the pepper pot, rearranged them on their tray and then put them back as they had been before. She was aware that Harry was happy to wait, giving her time to get her still sore emotions in order. There seemed to be an empathy between them, each knew what the other was thinking or feeling.

'A simple, sordid reason,' she said, her voice shaking only slightly. 'I caught him with another woman.'

'A shock,' Harry agreed, 'but sadly not an uncommon one.'

'I'll say it was a shock! And in my bed, too! I came home in the middle of the day—which I never used to do, but I'd forgotten some papers. I heard sounds in the bedroom, went in and there they were.'

She laughed. 'It was a shock for me—but a double one for them.'

Harry's voice was gentle. 'You appear to find

something genuinely funny,' he said. 'That is unusual.'

'There was something—not funny, but grotesque. It was the woman my partner was with. Martha Smythe. Known behind her back as Smarty Marty. She was Robin's professor and his consultant. She was at least twenty years older than him. And I'm going to be catty. She was—is—ugly.'

Harry was a good listener. She knew he was trying to keep the tone between them light, stopping her from getting too emotional. At the moment, high emotion between them just wasn't right. 'Being catty may be wrong but it's very enjoyable,' he said. 'Now, tell me the grotesque part of the story.'

'It was Robin's attitude! He thought it was my fault, was angry with me. He said that he still loved me but that sleeping with his professor would help his career! And now she would be angry with him. Did I want that?'

'And after that your life together was at an end?'

'From that very moment. I moved into hospital accommodation the same day. But Robin just couldn't understand why. When I told him I was moving out at once he was hurt, and shocked and dismayed.'

'Hurt, shocked and dismayed,' said Harry. 'Things don't get much worse than that.'

'You be careful. You might be making fun of my almost broken heart,' she pointed out.

'I might be. But I— Ah, light conversation is now at an end. This is serious stuff.'

'My love life isn't serious?' she asked, mock-angrily.

'Very serious. Tragic even. But I've always found that a good meal makes tragedy easier to bear.'

Two more plates were placed in front of them. On each was a vast steak. There were side dishes of salad and chips. Kim looked at the feast in wonder.

'I had intended to be ladylike,' she said, 'to order something light and dainty, like an omelette. But I was hungry and I dearly love chips. Besides, I'm a big girl.'

'I'll not comment on that,' he said.

The steak was grilled to perfection, the chips were light and the salad fresh. At the end of the meal Kim felt at peace with the world. She sipped her wine and said, 'I really enjoyed that. It was self-indulgent, but I'm starting a new job and I think I'm entitled to indulge myself. And I've told you all about Robin and I feel better for it. Isn't that odd?'

She couldn't quite understand his expression. He seemed perplexed. But all he said was, 'If I've helped you in any way, I'm glad.'

Then he handed her the menu. 'There's the ice cream to come,' he said.

So they ate the ice cream and afterwards they sat outside in the garden and drank coffee.

'I feel that all is well with life,' she said, 'so, being me, I'm going to start stirring things up. I've told you the important things about me, now I want to know about you. Are you the department wolf, Harry? Because I'm not a defenceless sheep. I can look after myself.'

'I've no doubt about that. And I don't think of you as a sheep—though if I did I'd offer to be your shepherd.'

'I'm sure you would. And I'm going to need quite a bit of shepherding at work, I don't know much about SCBU. But otherwise I can just see you in a long white smock, holding a crook and chewing a straw.'

'An attractive picture. It would certainly create confidence in the parents in the unit.'

'Confidence,' she said. 'How old are you, Harry?'

'I'm thirty-three. Why?'

She thought a moment. 'Earlier you said that you were feckless and fancy-free. I still want to know why you aren't in any kind of permanent relationship.'

He thought for a moment. 'For a couple who have only just met, we seem to be asking each other the most intimate questions.'

She realised he wasn't challenging her. He was accepting it, was as curious as to what had happened as she was. So she would push things a bit further. It might alter their relationship for good, but she just had to know.

'Harry, this morning you spilled coffee down me and I shouted at you, and then we actually looked at each other for the first time. What happened?'

'Well, I suggested that you change into—'

'Harry, don't mess me about! You know very well what I'm talking about. I felt it and I saw in your eyes that you felt it, too. What happened?'

It was getting dark now, shadows were creeping across the lawns around them and suddenly there were tiny lights illuminating the paths across the lawns. But it was still light enough to see his expression. She leaned across the table, stared at him intently.

For a moment she thought she caught a hint of dismay, of fear even. But then the old bland expression came back and she knew that whatever he said would be controlled, carefully worked out. He wasn't as impulsive as she was. However, he knew what she was talking about and his answer was possibly honest.

'I saw one of the most attractive girls I'd seen in months. Perhaps you were attracted to me, I hope so. It's not lightning striking, Kim, it's not a sudden divine revelation, it's not magic. It's the simple operation of hormones in our bodies, testosterone in mine and oestrogen in yours. Mother Nature wants the species to reproduce so she arranges this kind of reaction.'

'You're just one of the world's romantics, aren't you? Hormones indeed!'

But he had acknowledged that he knew what she was talking about. And she didn't think he was completely certain of his answer.

'You know hormones are important. They govern our actions, our feelings, the way we see the world.'

'Perhaps. But there are other things.'

Kim thought that she had taken things far enough. She detected an unease in Harry, he didn't like talking about his feelings. Well, she could wait. She yawned, glanced at her watch. 'Harry, I'd better be getting back. This conversation isn't finished—in fact, it's only just starting. But there'll be other times. Now, I've really enjoyed this evening but I'm bushed and I could do with a good night's sleep.'

'Of course.' He stood, offered her his hand to help her up. 'Are we still friends?'

'Of course we are,' she said. 'But, one last thing. I can guess that all your instincts as a gentleman are against it, but I want you to stay here. I want to walk back to my place alone, you know I'll be quite safe.'

'My instincts as a gentleman are against it,' he said.

'Too bad. For once you'll have to ignore them.'

She leaned over, kissed him quickly on the cheek, then walked purposefully away into the gathering dusk.

For a moment Harry considered following her. Then he decided it wouldn't be a good idea. There was a toughness in Kim that suggested she didn't like being ignored. He had already paid the bill, accepting after a small argument that she could pay for the wine. Now he walked back into the bar and bought himself a pint of beer. There were a couple of people he knew there, he could easily have walked over and chatted for an hour or so. But he didn't want to chat. He wanted—he needed—to think.

When he had got up this morning his life had been in order. He'd known what his ambitions were, where he was going. Then he had received the news that he had the position in Australia—that had been fantastic, and even now as he thought of it he got a buzz of satisfaction. He was on his way.

Then Kim had arrived. And he'd known at once that things were going to be different.

He had given her a plausible, semi-scientific explanation of what had happened between them. But he knew it wasn't enough. All doctors learned very quickly that science couldn't explain everything about human behaviour. He had told her that what had happened between them wasn't magic. The trouble was, it seemed like magic.

What was he going to do? He just didn't know. He only knew that Kim was the first woman he had met for many years who was capable of disrupting his carefully arranged lifestyle. And he wasn't too happy about it. But he thought he could probably treat her as he'd treated his other girlfriends. Tell her from the start that this was to be a purely casual affair.

Kim did her two-day induction without going back to the unit. Then she phoned Chris, who told her that for a further three days she was to observe, to spend some time with Harry, to watch what the nurses as well as the doctors did, and the following week she'd be put to work.

'Sounds good to me,' she said. She was looking forward to it.

She was there the next morning, neat in her white coat and with her hair tied well back. Chris introduced her to the team that was on duty and then suggested she might like to watch Jane for a couple of hours.

'As you know, Jane and I are engaged,' he told her. 'I'm not sure I approve of couples being too…close and working together. But for some reason there seems to have been quite a lot of romance in this department recently.'

'It's something in the air,' Jane told him, then

turned and winked at Kim. 'Let's hope it's not catching.'

'It won't infect me,' Kim said, 'I've had enough romance for a while. Now all I want to do is work.'

'Where have I heard that before?' Jane wondered. 'Any special reason for being anti-romance?'

'I just need a rest from it,' Kim said.

'Well, never mind. Come on and we'll look round for an hour or so.'

It was a while before Kim worked out what Jane was doing. Together they stood and looked at a baby in her incubator, then Jane said, 'This is baby Collins. She was born at thirty weeks, but she's been here three weeks now and we're pleased with her progress. I'll just have her out, change her nappy, give her a little wash. Why don't you watch?'

So Kim watched, recognising the skill with which Jane handled the baby, also recognising the affection Jane showed. And Jane crooned or talked to the baby as she worked.

'Babies like being talked to,' she told Kim. 'Best of all they like their mothers to talk to them—after all they've been listening to them for weeks in the womb. But any gentle voice will do. It calms them, makes them feel wanted.'

Kim watched carefully as Jane handled the minuscule body, noting how she spread her hands, how she never allowed the head to flop. Then baby Collins was put back in her incubator.

They moved on to the next baby. 'Johnny Wilkes,' said Jane. 'He's bigger and stronger than baby Collins. Why don't you take him out, wash him and change his nappy?'

So, very carefully, Kim did as she was asked. She realised that she was being shown more than the nurse's view of baby care. She was being given an introduction to the everyday handling of their tiny charges. And it was very worthwhile.

She quickly realised how much more skill Jane had than she did. But she would learn. And when she had finished, placed the dozing Johnny back in his incubator, she asked, 'Who thought of starting me like this? I think it's a great idea.'

Jane laughed. 'Chris would say that it's my idea and I think that it's his,' she said. 'When you get close to someone it's hard to decide who first thinks of something.'

'I've never been that close to anyone,' Kim muttered to herself regretfully.

In the afternoon Harry wandered in. She had wondered how he would greet her when they met again. She saw that he had decided to be casual, to carry on as if they were just two friendly colleagues. Their intimate conversation in the Escott was to be ignored—for now. Probably a good idea while they were in the unit. But there was a gleam in his eye, a little extra pressure on her shoulder when he guided her into the nursery. The conversation was not forgotten.

He invited her to come with him as he inspected one of their charges who was causing some anxiety. They looked down at a baby who, even to Kim's inexperienced eye, looked large, puffy even. Harry studied the monitors, invited Kim to do the same.

'Poor Benjamin here had a diabetic mother,' Harry

explained. 'The obs and gynae team did what they could, monitoring her insulin almost hour by hour. But suddenly her BP rocketed, there was imminent danger of pre-eclampsia so they decided on a Caesarean. So Benjamin survived but he's hypoglaecemic, his blood sugar is always too low. So we give it to him through his IV line. But then we have to make sure he doesn't get too much glucose. It's a constant battle, deciding on the precise amount to give him.'

'Surely you have tables to work out how much to give?'

'Certainly there are tables, based on body weight and past indications and so on. But there's no substitute for gut feeling. And I think Benjamin now needs a little more glucose.'

'Exactly why, Harry? I need to know, to learn.'

He thought for a moment then said, 'I look at Benjamin quite often. And I think he's showing more signs of distress than normal. Small signs but they're there. See the way he's wriggling, screwing up his face. You'll learn to spot them in time, Kim.'

'Fair enough,' she said, peering even closer at Benjamin. She realised that Harry was a conscientious and competent doctor. She would learn a lot from him—about medicine anyway.

'So how was your first week?' Harry asked late on Friday afternoon.

'I really enjoyed it,' she told him. 'But I'm looking forward to doing a bit on my own, to putting something back in instead of taking.'

'Don't worry, you'll get your chance. Now, I gather you've got the weekend off?'

'Yes. But Chris says this will be the last time for a while. After this I work the weekends—and the nights—on rotation like everyone else.'

'Welcome to the real world. D'you know about the party tomorrow night? At the hospital social club?'

'Yes. I've even bought a ticket. I gather we're trying to raise money to buy an extra scanner.'

'Well, that's the idea. In fact, I think it's just an excuse to have a party, which is fine by me. Do you have a partner for this shindig? A man to stand by your side, to protect you from the attentions of the madly dancing multitude?'

'I intend to be part of the madly dancing multitude,' she told him. 'And I don't need a partner or an escort, 'cos I'll be among friends, won't I? But if you're asking if you can call and accompany me there, the answer is yes. I'll sit at your table, we can share a bottle of wine again if you like. But I'm going there as one of the group. I've been made really welcome here.'

'Rejected,' he said gloomily. 'I shall have to watch you swirling in the arms of another and try to hide my grief.'

'Don't let it get you down. I'll save you every third waltz. Want to call round at my place at about eight? Then we can walk over together.'

'That'll be good,' he agreed. Then he looked at her assessingly. 'You want me to call at your flat? I think it's great but is there any special reason?'

'There might be, if I can think of one,' she told

him. 'But it certainly won't be the one that you possibly have in mind.'

'Bah, foiled!' he murmured.

Kim was quite looking forward to Saturday night. Tickets had been sold to anyone in the hospital, there was to be a disco and she had been told that the club was a great place to hold a party. And it was in aid of a very good cause. They were trying to raise money for a new scanner and recently the money hadn't been flowing in as quickly as was necessary. Kim sighed. She didn't mind giving something towards a scanner, but she thought it wrong that vital equipment should have to be bought by charitable appeals. Still…so long as the scanner appeared.

She was also looking forward to going with Harry. Just the thought of it excited her. But she felt she had to put a little distance between them—until she was sure how she and he both felt.

On Saturday morning she wandered round the little town. It was exciting, the long lengths of sand reminding her of holidays with her parents, when all she'd wanted to do had been to make castles with her bucket and spade. Different from large, industrial Sheffield. She found a large supermarket and bought a few things.

In the afternoon she studied. There were things she had seen that she didn't quite understand. Of course, she could and she would ask. But first she wanted to read up about her subject. It would make understanding easier.

Then it was time to prepare for the party.

She would wear a longish skirt in a dark burgundy

silk. It flattered her and it was cool. On top she would wear a white cotton blouse, draped down to her hips. She wanted to dance, she needed to be able to move.

She'd never taken too much time to dress and make-up, doctors just didn't have time. So she got ready for the party, then sat in one of the two easy chairs in her tiny lounge. On the coffee-table in front of her was a half bottle of red wine and two glasses. She'd also bought something called a party pack from the supermarket. A round plastic plate with compartments for nuts, crisps, olives, dried fruit and so on.

Nervously, she took a handful of nuts. She'd deliberately asked Harry to call for her, now she was wondering if it had been a good idea. But she felt they needed to talk again. And not in the intense atmosphere of the unit.

He rang her doorbell at precisely one minute to eight, she might have guessed that he'd be punctual. When she answered the door he thrust a sheaf of flowers towards her. They were sweet peas. She loved them. 'I was walking through the park,' he said, 'and I decided to pick these for you. I would have got you more but the park-keeper was chasing me.'

'Harry, they're lovely. And you're an idiot. Park-keeper indeed! Come on in and sit down while I put them in water.'

He was dressed in the same smart casual mode as herself. Black trousers with the sheen that suggested mohair, a beautifully cut silver-grey shirt. Does he know that the shirt reflects the colour of his eyes? she wondered. Did he buy it himself—or did a woman buy it for him? It's the kind of thing that a woman would look for. She found the idea of a woman buying things for Harry was rather unsettling.

She found a vase, put in the flowers and carried them through into the lounge. Harry stood as she entered.

'I see we're having a little party of our own,' he said, indicating the wine and the party plate. 'If you'd told me I would have brought some wine myself.'

'No need, I bought just half a bottle, not because I'm mean but because we're not staying here too long. Now, sit down and we'll chat a while.'

She leaned over, poured two glasses of wine. 'And help yourself to a nut or something.'

'I think I'll nibble an olive or two,' he murmured. 'I suspect I'll need the strength. Kim, I've got a bad feeling about all this. My old headmaster used to invite us into his study for what he called a little chat, and it was never a pleasant experience. Mind you, no wine or olives. Just cups of tea if you were lucky.'

'You're burbling again,' she told him. 'You're to stop. You've got to help me because this is serious and difficult. I've watched you. You hide behind your jokes.'

'Oh, dear,' he said. 'And I came out to enjoy myself.'

'You still can. Now, drink your wine while I think about what I'm going to say.'

He nodded, then reached for his wine and sipped it. She saw his face was calm—it so often was. But those silver eyes followed every move that she made.

'You're really pleased about this job in Australia, aren't you?' she started.

It wasn't the question he had been expecting. 'Very pleased,' he said. 'I expect to learn a lot and I'm really looking forward to living out there. There's a lot to see and do.'

'You'll be there for the three years initially. But there's a good chance you might stay?'

'It's possible, if I get the job I want. Though I'd miss England.'

'And you're going just after Christmas?'

'I'll put my resignation in on the first of October. Then I'll be free from the first of January. But I've got some leave owing, I'll probably take it then.'

'Four and a half months before you go. Then I'll never see you again.'

She said it calmly, flatly. But the sentence seemed to hang between them, like a curse or a threat.

He took a while to reply. Then, his voice almost casual, he said, 'Medicine is still a small world, we might run into each other some time. But probably not for long.'

'I'm just getting things sorted out in my mind, Harry. And I have to start with that fact. After four and a half months I'll never see you again.'

'You've only known me for six days anyway,' he pointed out after a while.

'Does that matter?'

'Perhaps not.'

'I don't think it really matters that you're going to Australia,' she told him. 'I think you're hiding behind that, too. Because you're going to disappear, you just can't get serious with anyone.'

She could tell he was uncomfortable with this conversation, well, she was uncomfortable herself. At the same time they both reached for their wineglasses, their fingers touched and then both jerked back their hands.

'We seem to think alike in many ways,' he said. 'This serious conversation is thirsty work.'

'True.' They both drank and then she went on, 'This kind of fuss about apparently nothing is not like me. For a while I wondered if I was just on the rebound from Robin, but I don't think so. That was dead a long time ago. But I saw you, and something flared between us and since then it's got worse. It hits me when I see you by accident. For a while I even thought of asking for a transfer so I could get away from you, but I'm not going to. I'm not running, I've got to get over it.'

'I've never met anyone who is as honest as you,' he said. 'Don't you feel vulnerable, telling me about what you feel?'

'Yes, I do feel vulnerable. But it's something I've got to live with. Besides, whether rightly or not, I trust you.' She grinned. 'And don't make any mistake, Harry. I may be hurting but I'm not helpless.'

'Helpless is the last thing I'd call you. So, tell me, what do you want from me?'

'I think you're a kind man, so it's not much to ask. We work together. We can go to functions like tonight together. But you don't treat me as someone to amuse yourself with until you disappear to the other side of the world.'

He nodded thoughtfully. 'So no easy, no-strings-attached relationship for a few weeks? Seems fair, doesn't it? Since I'm a kind man it's not much to ask so I'll do what you say. But there's just one question, though.'

'I've been doing the talking so far. Take a turn.'

'What if I like your company, want to see more of you, hope that things can progress?'

'Harry, while you're going to Australia there's no future in it.'

'What happens if I'm hurting like you are?'

'That's too bad,' she said, 'but welcome to the club. And have another olive.'

CHAPTER THREE

IT WAS a great party.

She walked over to the hospital club with Harry, both of them enjoying the evening air. On the way they met Erica and Matt, Erica's fiancé, who also worked on the unit. Good, they could arrive as a small group.

There were more friends inside, they had commandeered a table of their own. Practically everyone from SCBU was there, the only exceptions being those who were on duty. They were a tightly knit group; Kim was becoming one of them and she liked it. There had been groups in other hospital departments that had been not only unfriendly but sometimes downright hostile.

She tried to make sure—for her own benefit and that of other people—that she wasn't just with Harry. She was sitting next to him, sharing a bottle of wine with him, but the conversation ranged cheerfully wide across the table. It was an occasion to let your hair down, and if you shouted a bit more than usual—who cared?

After a while the disco started and a few couples got up to dance. Kim decided to ask Harry if he would like to join her on the floor. All right, she'd just told him that in future they'd have to keep some distance between them. But dancing couldn't do any harm. And she loved it as she loved most physical exercise.

'I thought you'd never ask,' he said as he took her hand and led her onto the floor. 'Is this one of those new-fangled waltzes you told me about?'

'If it's too much for you, Grandad, you can lean on me,' she told him. 'Now, don't try to get both feet off the ground at the same time.'

Having said which, she should not have been surprised to see just how good a dancer he was.

Mind you, he didn't dance as she did. Unlike Kim, who threw herself into her dancing, Harry danced like the character he was—smoothly, rhythmically, always in control. They made a good, contrasting couple. She thought that they went so well together. Then she tried to forget the thought. It was good to dance again! She hadn't had the chance in months. This was to be a test. Could she enjoy herself with Harry and still remain detached from him? She thought she could.

After that she seemed to dance with every man at the table. She saw that Harry was equally popular, and it pleased her. But as they passed on the floor she saw him looking at her.

It was a good party. If the music the DJ played was a song, then everyone sang along—as loudly as possible. And Kim joined in. She liked singing nearly as much as dancing.

'You've a great voice,' one of the nurses told her cheerfully, 'plenty of power. D'you know the words to "I Will Survive"?'

'Used to sing it all the time during my exams. It cheered me up. Why?'

'Just curious,' the nurse said, with a small smile on her face. 'Now, don't go away.'

The almost continuous music stopped, the dancers trooped off the floor and the DJ put a microphone on a stand in front of his array of flashing lights. 'Ladies and gentlemen, this is a dance night, not a karaoke night, but we all remember the spirited singing we had at the last party here, and there have been requests for a repeat. Now, one of the ladies in question isn't here tonight. She's decided to have a baby instead.'

'No sense of priorities,' a voice shouted from the audience, and everyone laughed.

'Perhaps so. But the two ladies who remain have been conducting a long series of auditions and they believe they have found a replacement. A new recruit. Ladies and gentlemen, I give you the Anderson Grandchildren.'

There was more laughter, applause. Kim was looking on in interest when someone tapped her on the shoulder. It was the nurse who had spoken to her before. 'Come on,' said the nurse, 'we're on.'

'But...the Anderson Grandchildren...I can't...'

'You can, we just heard you. And you know the words. Come on, it's a party.'

Yes, it was a party. So she allowed herself to be led to the front of the stage, leaned towards the microphone and with the other two nurses belted out how she would survive. If she had to do it then she'd do it well—and judging by the applause at the end it was good enough.

There were shouts for more when they'd finished. But the DJ firmly said that he was sorry, time now for something much more important, refreshments were now being served. The main lights went on and Kim walked back to her table—to be applauded once again.

'That was good,' said Harry. 'You're a girl of many parts.'

'I just like singing.' She sat down, fanned her warm face. 'It's a song that appeals to me.'

'I could tell that. Will you survive, Kim Hunter?'

'That's my intention. Though I might get battered on the way.' She looked at him, realised that he knew what she was getting at. 'Harry, I will survive—even survive you. But now you're going to have to excuse me a minute—or fifteen. I've got to go to the ladies' and effect what they called running repairs. I must look a mess.'

'I think you look gorgeous as you are,' he said. 'But off you go.'

The ladies' was full but eventually she found herself a seat in front of a mirror. There she was congratulated on her singing again. 'Did you come here with Harry Black?' the girl sitting next to her asked.

'I'm new here,' Kim said carefully. 'I came with him but we're not really together or anything. He's just showing me round.'

'Really,' said the other girl, disbelievingly. 'I wish he'd just show me round.'

But it wasn't said nastily. Kim smiled and reached for her handbag.

Yes, she was enjoying herself. She thought she might have got the Harry situation under control. She could be with him, like him, enjoy his company. If he wanted more than that—well, too bad, she could cope. She thought of the song she had just sung so energetically. Yes, she would survive. Now, what had happened to the make-up she had applied so carefully?

Harry sat alone at the SCBU table, his fingers gently stroking the stem of his wineglass. The others had gone table-hopping or to queue for food. He would wait till Kim returned. He thought he was enjoying himself, if in a strange way. He couldn't throw himself into things as Kim did. But he loved to watch her enjoying herself.

After a couple of minutes he was joined by Chris, who accepted a glass of wine, agreed that it was a good do and that Kim had been fantastic as a singer.

'SHOs aren't usually as outgoing as Kim,' he said. 'They're too bothered with coping with the work and worrying about their exams. It's good to see someone who can do both.'

'Good indeed,' Harry said. 'I'm enjoying working with her.'

There was a pause and then Chris said, elaborately casual, 'She's only been here a week, Harry. Just how close are you getting to her?'

Harry looked at his friend. This was not a question he would take from anyone. But he would from Chris.

'I'm working with her,' he said, 'I like being with her. I hope I'm helping to teach her something.'

Chris took a mouthful of wine, obviously ill at ease. 'I've been pushed into this by my wife-to-be,' he said. 'She's spent some time with Kim, got to like her. She thinks that Kim isn't as confident as she seems. This is not my business but we all know…your relationships never seem to last. You'll be going soon and—'

'I'd be entirely entitled to tell you to mind your own business,' Harry said cheerfully. 'Kim is a big girl, I'm a big boy. But I know you're doing this out of concern for her and I appreciate it. So don't worry. I like her a lot and I'll see she's not hurt.'

He thought for a moment and added, 'But, Chris, I suspect she's tougher than you think. She can look after herself.'

Chris looked relieved. 'Am I glad this conversation is over,' he said. He stood. 'Let me fetch you a drink, Harry.'

Harry looked at him half-mockingly. 'Chris, before you go. Why did you assume that Kim was the one likely to get hurt? What about me?'

Chris winced. 'I just can't cope with this,' he said. 'You're upsetting all my preconceptions. Let's face it, Harry, when it comes to romance, everyone thinks of you as the iron man. Love them and gently leave them.'

'That's me,' said Harry.

He knew his reputation was deserved. He wondered if he was as pleased with it now as he had always been. Still, it was something to hide behind.

Kim thought she'd done a good job. In ten minutes she'd managed to return her appearance to the way it had been when she'd first walked into the club, cool and collected.

Harry rose to meet her when she arrived back at the table. 'Once again, you look very chic,' he said.

'If a man might use a word like chic. But I'm not sure I didn't prefer you looking wild and rather frightening, as you did when you were singing.'

'Both bits of the real me. Now, can we go to eat? I'm ravenous.' Then she frowned. 'Didn't I say that the last time we went out together?'

'It's not a fault. And I shan't say anything about girls with appetites.'

They joined the queue, took a plateful of food each. The club buffet was excellent. They took their plates back to the table and chatted with those of the others who weren't table-hopping.

Before the dancing started again there was the draw for the raffle. Both of them had bought a book of tickets as they'd come in and waited hopefully for one of their numbers to come up. There was a table full of prizes—all of them donated.

In the end it was Harry who won. He went to the table, chose a big box of chocolates and when he returned he said smugly, 'People will think that I'm going to give these to you. But I'm not. I'm going to keep them.'

'If I win I'm going to pick that big teddy that nobody else wants,' she said. 'And I will give it to you and you'll have to keep it on your bed.'

He winced. 'Have a chocolate,' he said.

Perhaps it was a good thing that she didn't win.

This was technically a fundraising event so after a while the chairman of the scanner committee made a small speech, saying that they had done well tonight but that they were still a little under target. He knew many people had done a lot of good work but with just one more push they should raise the full amount of money.

'I know I've got plenty on,' she told Harry, 'but if there's something I could do, I'd like to.'

'Good. I'm sure there'll be something.' He looked at her speculatively. 'You know I'm on the scanner committee?'

That surprised her. 'You never told me. I wouldn't have thought you were a committee sort of man.'

'I'm not. But sometimes… Carrying on with my policy of taking you to every drinking den in town, I'd like you to come to the Fisherman's Arms. They're organising a big knockout darts competition in a week or so, teams from most local pubs, and we get the profits. I'll be there and I could do with a gofer and a results clerk.'

'This is so romantic. No one's ever asked me to be a gofer at a darts competition before.'

'It's like being an SHO, only worse. You do all the work and get none of the thanks.'

'You've talked me into it,' she said. 'Now, can we dance again?'

She was pleased that he had asked to go somewhere where they could work together. She could deal with that.

So, it had been a good party. She had survived—no trouble from Harry or herself. Afterwards he walked her home through the still warm night, they talked casually about work and he didn't try to hold her hand. But when he took her arm to guide her down a short-cut, she felt herself tingle at his touch. In spite

of what she had said to him, he still had the power
to excite her, whether she wanted him to or not.

Finally they were at her front door, and she could
feel his uncertainty. He was holding back, not sure
exactly what to do. Well, she was a little uncertain
herself. She unlocked her door, turned to him.

'Good night, Kim, it's been lots of fun being with
you.'

'In spite of the gloomy talk we had to start with.
It's been fun being with you, too, Harry.'

She just couldn't help it, she leaned forward to kiss
him—on the cheek, of course. A polite good-night
kiss. But somehow she kissed him on the lips. It was
nice, it couldn't hurt, they'd got things sorted out
between them, it was only a kiss after all. But it
lasted.

And then she found his arms round her, her arms
were round him and a good-night kiss had turned into
something much more dangerous. But it was so
good...

And it ended so suddenly. He took his arms from
round her, moved away from her. She could sense
the effort it took him. They were still close, but apart,
and harshly he said, 'I think that's probably enough,
don't you?'

A silence that seemed far longer than it really was.
'Probably enough,' she agreed. 'Good night, Harry.'
Then she ran inside.

She stood just inside the door, and after a moment
heard the diminishing sound of his footsteps as he
walked away down the path.

Moving automatically, she undressed, hung up her
clothes, showered, cleaned her teeth and then sat with

her cocoa and the inevitable digestive biscuit. And then she had to think.

She thought things had gone well for most of the evening. He had accepted what she'd had to say before they'd gone out. They had reached an understanding, they could be close but not too close. They had enjoyed themselves—together and with others—at the party. And then she had kissed him. That had ruined all her good work, all her good intentions. For a moment she felt warm as she relived the rush of emotions she had felt. But even though she knew she wasn't being fair to herself, she had been unable to resist.

Then something slightly unsettling struck her. She hadn't finished the kiss. *He* had. He had been the one who'd been strong, had done what she'd asked him. Was this to be the pattern of things to come? She hoped not. She had to be tough herself.

Whatever they might feel for each other, neither was going to let it interfere with their work. Two days later they were side by side, looking down at one of their charges. 'I'm not very happy about the way baby Perkins here is behaving,' Harry said. He stuck his finger into the incubator and stroked the tiny pink hand. 'He seems healthy enough, but his temperature is fluctuating more than I like.'

He looked at the notes clipped to the bottom of the incubator. 'I can't remember what happened last week.'

'I'll go and fetch last week's notes,' Kim volunteered. 'You carry on a minute.'

She left the little nursery, walked quickly down

the corridor. 'Kim, are you working with Harry?' a nurse called. 'Will you tell him there's just been a phone call, an urgent personal message, no name given. But will he ring this number as quickly as he can?' She handed Kim a slip of paper.

'I'll tell him at once,' Kim said, but found baby Perkins's notes first. She knew this was what Harry would want.

Typically, Harry looked at the notes first, and decided there was no real cause for worry over baby Perkins, but they would review him the next day. 'An urgent personal phone call,' he said, and looked thoughtfully at the slip of paper Kim had handed him. 'I don't recognise the number. It must be a desperate bank manager. Or perhaps the Queen wants to ennoble me for services to medicine and helping young SHOs. How does Sir Harry Black sound to you?'

'It has a definite ring,' she told him. 'Now, I'll leave you alone in the doctors' room to make your urgent personal call and I'll make us both a fresh coffee.'

'That sounds a great plan.'

She made the coffee, sat and waited. But Harry didn't appear. After ten minutes she decided that it must be a long and boring business call and Harry wouldn't mind if she took the coffee into him. So she knocked on the door then opened it. 'Harry, I've brought you... Is everything all right?'

He had finished his telephone call and was sitting white-faced, staring at nothing. She had never seen the imperturbable Harry look so stricken.

He didn't answer her, so after a moment's hesitation she went over and took his arm. Gently, she shook it. 'Harry, are you all right?'

Somehow he dragged himself back from where he had been, managed a feeble smile. 'I'm fine. I...I just banged into the side of the desk, must have hit a nerve or something. It'll be all right in a minute.'

She looked at him but didn't say that she didn't believe him. 'I thought you'd had bad news on the telephone.'

'No! That...that was nothing.'

She fetched the coffee over to him. 'Why don't you drink this coffee and I'll finish the round? There isn't anything I can't deal with.'

'Yes...if you would finish the round. But I think I'll go for a walk outside. I've got my pager with me, don't hesitate to call if there's anything, I'll only be ten minutes.'

'Do you want me to—?'

'I'll be fine, Kim,' he said, but there was a flatness in his voice that she had never heard before.

He appeared to drink the hot coffee in one gulp, then walked out of the door without further comment. She watched his disappearing back with dismay, she'd never seen him so down. One thing, she knew that the story about hurting his side was rubbish. What had he heard on the telephone?

She tried to persuade herself that it was none of her business, but she couldn't. Now she had a...regard for Harry. She wondered. Then after a moment she went to carry on with the round.

He came back ten minutes later, cheerfully told her that his side was better, they'd get on with the work. But there was strain and unease under the cheerfulness. He was more silent than usual. She knew he was hurting.

She tried again after a while. 'So your telephone message wasn't serious?'

'Not serious, nothing to worry about.'

He knew that she knew he was keeping something from her, it was obvious from his face. But he was entitled to secrecy, to his dignity. She didn't push it further. But she would have liked it if he had confided in her. She wanted to help.

They worked together for a while in more or less companionable silence. And then something else struck her. Why was she so concerned—worried even—about a man who she needed to be only a casual friend? And the answer to her question came, an almost shocking revelation that she couldn't avoid. She…cared for Harry more than she liked to admit. She refused to think that her feelings might even be stronger than this.

This was lunacy! Really, she knew nothing at all about Harry Black.

She didn't know that things were about to change.

CHAPTER FOUR

It HAPPENED a couple of days later. Harry opened the door to the doctors' room and said casually, 'Got any time free tonight?'

'I've got a couple of hours. Why?'

'I'm being a good mover. Since I'm going to Oz, I'm going to get rid of my life here. I've started on my books. I can only take so many, a lot will go to the charity shops. I thought you might find something useful in the rest. Want to come round and look? About eightish?'

Her first reaction was that she did very much want to go round to his flat. It would perhaps tell her a bit more about him. But how would that make her feel? Still… 'Give me the address,' she said. 'And eight will be fine.'

I've always travelled light, Harry thought as he walked down the corridor, I'm not much interested in possessions. For that matter, I've not been too interested in most of the relationships that I've had. It will be easy to get rid of my life here. And when Kim sees the steps I've taken, the cardboard boxes I've filled with stuff to throw out, it'll make her realise that I really am going. And that can't be a bad thing. I don't want to hurt her.

But he knew that his principal emotion was one

59

of pleasure at thinking of her in his home. Then he tried to force himself to stop thinking that way.

Harry had a flat in a small block in a pleasant tree-lined suburb about a mile from the hospital. Kim parked Bessie, rang the bell marked with his name. There was a buzz, the door opened and a disembodied voice said, 'I live on the top floor. There is a lift but for health's sake I always walk. Take your pick.'

'I'll walk,' she said.

He was waiting for her in his open doorway. 'Welcome to Harry Black Towers,' he said, bowing. 'I trust your visit will be a happy one.'

'I trust you've hoovered and made the bed,' she said. ''Cos I'm going to be nosy like you and have a look round. And like you I'm going to call it intellectual curiosity.'

He stepped back, waved her in. 'My home is yours,' he said.

She stood in the hall and looked round with some interest. 'It's a nice flat in a nice area,' she said. 'Are you going to sell it?'

'Not mine to sell. I've leased it and the lease is nearly up. I've never bought a property.'

'Because you've never wanted to settle?'

'Something like that,' he said. 'Now, the conducted tour. Down this corridor we have the living room, the study, the dining room, conservatory and library.' He opened a door. 'That's this room here.'

Her first reaction was that he'd been completely wrong when he'd said that he never wanted to settle down. This was the room of a home-maker. It was decorated and lit to make its small size less obvious.

There was a wooden floor with a couple of rich red Persian rugs. On one wall was a set of Gillray prints. There was no clutter, the furniture sparse but elegant. An oak desk with the inevitable computer largely hidden. A director's chair. A two-seater leather couch and a coffee-table that matched the floor. All was neat and tidy. The only discordant note was the bookcase that ran along one wall. There were half-filled cardboard boxes along the bottom of it.

'The boxes are for what I want to take,' he said. 'The rest I have to dispose of. Now, shall we continue our tour?'

The bathroom was full of plants. The kitchen was neat, with a tiny dining space at one end. There was a calendar pinned to one wall and a shelf of cookery books.

'Do you have a cleaning lady?' she asked. 'It's all very neat.'

'No. I do it all myself. I like to be self-sufficient.'

She filed that remark away in her mind, to be considered later. 'And the bedroom?' she asked.

He raised his eyebrows but said nothing.

She shivered as she entered. This was different again. There was a double bed, plain white pillows and duvet cover. The walls were white, there were no curtains, only white venetian blinds. Along one wall were built-in cupboards and drawers—also in white.

'Like the room?' he asked.

'I don't know. I can't make up my mind whether it's clinical or virginal.'

He laughed. 'Neither of those. I wanted a room

where I could sleep without any external stimulus whatsoever.'

'I see,' she said. 'You have difficulty in sleeping?'

'Never.'

Had his answer held just a little too much conviction?

She looked at the book on his—white—bedside table. It was a guide to Australia. Just one thing to read. By the side of her bed there must have been a couple of dozen books.

'I wanted to see your home because I think that where people live tells us more about their character than almost anything else,' she said frankly. 'Now I've seen your home I'm more confused than ever. Did you design all this yourself? Was there any other influence? Girlfriends perhaps?'

He laughed. 'You know me better than that. Any girlfriend wanting to show a home-building instinct in this flat would be quickly shown the door. It's a one-man flat, all my own work.'

He took her arm, led her out of the bedroom. 'Come and start looking through my books while I get us something to drink. Coffee or tea?'

She realised he wanted her to talk about books, not ask him about his home-building. 'I'd like coffee, please,' she said.

His books were fascinating, they showed what wide-ranging interests he had. There were medical books, of course—but most of them he was taking with him. There were novels, both modern and nineteenth-century, histories of architecture, biographies of scientists. And sets of guides to the counties.

She reached for a guide to Cumbria, high on the

top shelf, and called out, 'Do you go to the Lake District much?'

A voice came from the kitchen. 'Not for years. I used to, but now I prefer Wales.'

She opened the book, it had that not unattractive smell of unopened books. As she stepped back she dropped the book and it landed open, the cover ballooning upwards. Irritated, she reached down for it, hoping that none of the pages had come adrift. It was intact. But inside the front cover, which had been stuck down with clear tape, she saw the edge of a photograph. She opened the book again, shook it and the photograph fell out.

It was an old black and white photograph. There was a background of mountains. Posing happily, arms round each other, were two figures in boots and walking gear. One was Harry—younger certainly but with that unmistakable smile. The other was a girl, smiling at him, dark-haired and attractive.

Harry came in carrying a tray and the coffee smelled so good. He placed the tray on the table and she held out the picture to him. 'This seems like a nice girl. Who is she?' Then, instantly, she regretted what she had done.

His easy-smiling face went blank. He stood perfectly still, staring at the picture. Then, hoarsely, he asked, 'Where did you get that?'

'It fell out when I dropped this book on the floor.'

He took the photograph from her, glanced at it once and then methodically tore it into small pieces. The pieces he dropped into a waste-paper basket. 'Just an old girlfriend,' he said when he had finished. 'I haven't thought of her in years. Didn't know the photo was there. Now, there's coffee here and, knowing you, I've even bought some digestive biscuits. What books have you chosen so far?'

She looked at him. There were questions that she wanted to ask about the girl, but she knew it wasn't a good idea. 'I'd like to talk to you about this old girlfriend,' she said, 'but now isn't the time, is it?'

'Not really.' He looked at her with that perfectly calm expression that sometimes she thought she could hate.

So she sat by him on the couch and drank her coffee. 'I saw that book by your bedside about Australia,' she said. 'Tell me about the place.'

He settled back in his place with relief. 'I'm going to Perth. It's a great city with wonderful beaches. Of the fifteen most poisonous snakes in the world, eleven are to be found in Oz.'

'You make it sound so attractive.'

'It is. Sometimes you get a big brown in your garden. It's deadly if it's disturbed. So you send for the council and they collect your big brown and take it miles into the desert and leave it to walk back home.'

'Snakes don't walk, they wriggle.'

'Whatever. And have I told you about the poisonous spiders that live under lavatory seats? The funnel web spider is one of the most venomous insects in the world.'

'That's enough wildlife,' she said decidedly. 'We've established that you've got a death wish. And, please, don't start on the giant sharks. Now, what's this pure research you're going to do? I thought you loved the hands-on work with neonates.'

'I do. And I get the chance to keep it up. But this

Ph.D programme I'm on is dealing with the growth of the early foetus, we're trying to find out what genetic misalignment causes abnormalities to develop. What manages to cross through the placenta. There will be no practical results straight away, but in ten or twenty years my tiny bit of research might help a child to survive that otherwise would have died.'

'That's important to you, isn't it?'

'Well, yes. But more important is the fact that with a Ph.D I shall be a doctor twice over. I told you, I shall insist on being addressed as Dr Doctor.'

He drank his coffee. 'I believe Perth is a lovely place. Are you sure there's no chance of you visiting Australia in the next two or three years? You could drop in on me.'

This was a dangerous question. If she said yes it would raise all sorts of difficult problems between them. So she said, 'No. I'll finish my training and then I'll become a GP. No time for gallivanting across the world. If you want to see more of me you'll have to stay in England.'

'It's good to know exactly what you want to do,' he said, ignoring what she'd said about England. 'Now, have you picked any books you'd like?'

There were many that she would like, but she refused to take more than a box full. He offered her the Gillray prints, said that he certainly didn't want to take them. She agreed she would accept them— but only days before he left. Then she said she had to leave, she was on early the next day.

Perhaps it was her fault. They were standing in the hall, the box of books on the floor between them. And she reached out to kiss him.

It was intended to be just a polite little thing. A courtesy between friends. She leaned over the box, took him lightly by the arms and moved to kiss him.

And first she said, 'This is just a thank-you kiss. Thank you for the books, for showing me round your flat, for the conversation. Just a thank-you kiss.'

'What else?' he asked. 'But not a thank-you kiss like last time?'

She felt a thrill of apprehension. Last time, after the party, that had started as a good-night kiss. And then it had changed, how it had changed.

But she kissed him anyway—and she was lost. The touch of his lips was gentle at first, but soon became deeper, more intense, and there was nothing she could do. She gave herself to him.

She knew nothing but the touch, the feel of him. In her urge to be close to him she tripped over the box of books, would have sprawled on the floor. But he held her, pulled her close to him and she was supported. Her breasts were crushed to his chest, she could feel the length of his thighs against hers.

He kicked the box aside, books spilled from it and they were fully together. Without knowing how, she found her arms round his neck, the tips of her fingers caressing the muscles, the pulse that beat in his throat. And he held her tight with one arm and with the other he stroked her back, a gentle, rhythmic, soothing motion that both calmed and excited her.

Just for a moment fear flashed through her mind. She had decided that this was not the thing that she needed. A kiss, certainly. But not this warmth, this languor that stretched through her entire body. Not this feeling of contentment, this feeling of certainty that, whatever he wanted, she would want it, too.

For a minute or an hour they remained in the hall, locked together. Then he slid one arm further round her waist and urged her to come with him. She could not resist. He led her into his bedroom.

There was no light, only the last rays of the setting sun casting an orange glow across the room.

How had it happened? They were sitting side by side on his bed and his kisses increased in urgency, an urgency that she felt, too. Willingly, her mouth opened under the onslaught of his tongue. With a sigh she lay backward. There was no hurry. All would be well. Harry would see to that. Now his hands were easing her shirt upwards, opening the buttons, feeling for her half-cup bra. When he leaned over her to kiss the slopes of her breasts she sighed in anticipation. Whatever he wanted, she wanted as well.

He left her. Suddenly there were no hands touching her, no searching lips, no arms around her. Her half-closed eyes flicked open, her brow creased. 'Harry, where are you, what are you doing?' she asked fretfully.

She sensed him walk to the other side of the double bed, throw himself onto it. But he didn't reach for her. Turning her head, she saw him lying stiff on his back, staring at the ceiling. 'What's wrong?' she asked.

This time her voice was calm, even cold. Somehow she concealed the churning of her feelings, the vast hurt and disappointment.

'What do you want of me, Kim?' he asked. His

voice also was calm, but she could sense the mael-
strom of emotions underneath.

'I would have thought that was obvious. Isn't it
what you want, too?' This time she could not disguise the pain in her voice.

'I guess we want the same thing now. But what
will you want tomorrow?'

It took a while to work out what he was asking,
to think through the various replies that were true
and yet not too revealing. In the end she said, 'I'll
want you.' A simple, honest statement.

'How long will you want me for?'

'For as long as it lasts. As long as it takes. And,
Harry, don't start telling me that you're going to
Australia. You're using that as an excuse. If…if…
eventually we felt that we meant something to each
other, well, we could deal with Australia. It's a problem but not an insoluble one.'

'True. The problem is me. I just don't do…long-
term relationships.'

'Harry, that's just plain stupid! You're a mature
man, not a teenager in thrall to his hormones. You
can make decisions, there's nothing more pathetic
than a grown man wandering through life, picking
up woman after woman.'

'That's telling me,' he said. 'What would you want
of me?'

Somehow she had got the better of her temper. 'I'd
want you to acknowledge that…in time…there might
be a relationship that could grow between us,' she
said. 'Perhaps it won't. I've been hurt and disappointed before, you might be, too. But at least I'd be
willing to try. Why can't you try?'

'You asked me to keep my distance,' he pointed out. 'You wanted a man-free six months.'

'And things changed. They do. But it looks like I'll get my six man-free months anyway. Or I could sleep with you, Harry, and carry on sleeping with you till you're ready to go. Then at the appointed time off you go to Australia, send me a postcard or two, and I'm one of a line of half-forgotten women.'

'It's the way I am,' he said, his voice harsh.

'Then I feel nearly as sorry for you as I do for myself.'

Both lay there, nearly touching and yet miles apart. Then something curious struck her. 'Harry,' she said, her voice now tentative, 'you started this. You stopped what we were doing, you almost picked a fight with me. Did you do that for me?'

'I do have a bit of a conscience,' he said, 'though I desperately wanted to sleep with you.'

Kim sighed, sat up and carefully rebuttoned her shirt. 'That's the difference between us,' she said. 'You wanted to sleep with me. I wanted to make love with you. Harry, I'll take my books and go.'

She couldn't help herself. She leaned over, quickly kissed him on the lips. 'You could be a loveable man, Harry Black.'

Then she picked up her box of books and went.

Harry stood at his bedroom window and watched Bessie rattle into life then chug away down the street. Then walked to his living room and poured himself a drink.

He had hoped to frighten Kim off, to make her realise that he was leaving, that there could be nothing between them. And it had all ended in farce. How he had wanted her! He hoped she appreciated that.

He sipped his whisky. He had intended to make more decisions about his future, decide what else he could dispose of. Never before had he felt any difficulty in throwing things away. But now he was finding decisions hard to make. He wandered from room to room, looking around his little flat. He had been—he still was—comfortable here. And he was remembering how Kim's presence had lit up the place. He wondered what his flat would be like in Australia. He wondered if he'd find someone like Kim to light it up. He thought probably not. Did that bother him? Well, yes, it did. He was getting too fond of Kim.

Irritated at the way his thoughts were moving, he took the coffee-tray out of the living room. Then, even more irritated, he picked out the bits of the torn-up photograph from the basket. He flushed them down the lavatory.

Kim went back to her flat, not knowing what to think. She felt out of sorts, not sure what she really wanted but sure of what she didn't want. She didn't want Harry to go to Australia. But the sight of him packing had made that even more certain. Perhaps she would look through the books he had given her—when she saw his signature on the fly sheet she felt worse than ever.

At first it was uncomfortable seeing Harry next morning. 'I've just been chatting to Chris,' he said to her. 'I gather you've offered to work through to

midnight tonight and you're having the afternoon off?'

She shrugged. 'I'm happy to be flexible. It suits
Chris and I don't mind when I work.'

'So have you any plans for this afternoon?'

It was the way he asked that made her curious.
Usually he spoke to her in the cheerful joking voice
that he used with everyone. But this time he seemed
unsure, almost hesitant.

'Nothing special arranged. Certainly nothing that
I can't put off. Why? Are you offering to take me
out?'

She had spoken flippantly, she felt both sorry and
surprised when she saw what seemed like pain in his
eyes. But all he said was, 'Sort of. We'll go for a
drive for a couple of hours. Pick you up at your place
at two o'clock? No need to wear anything special but
make sure you're warm.'

Now she was curious. 'What sort of a drive,
Harry? Where are we going?'

'We're going to see my past,' he said. Then he
walked away.

He called for her promptly at two. He smiled at
her but it wasn't the usual cheerful grin and she felt
his mind was elsewhere. She was both intrigued and
apprehensive. He had said they would go to see his
past. Whatever she was to see, she felt that this meeting might help to explain the enigma that was Harry
Black. How she would feel about him afterwards, she
wasn't sure.

They took the road out of Denham up into the
Wolds. He'd been right, it was cold. The sun was

out but it was bleak, and there was a wind that cut through to the bone.

The road was largely deserted, there was an occasional tractor but very little else. Harry was silent, even sombre. She decided to give him time, to let him speak when he was ready. Again, she felt that this meeting with him would be pivotal in their relationship. Things could go any number of ways.

After a while he said, 'I've been at Denham two and a half years now. I came here deliberately—it had a good reputation—but I could have gone to a bigger hospital in Leeds or Glasgow. And now I'm moving on. I think.'

'You mean you had a special reason for coming here? Not a medical one?'

'You could say that. I needed to get away from big towns.' They drove another mile or two in silence. She desperately wanted to ask questions but had decided not to try and force the conversation. Obviously he had something to say and he must do it in his own time. She felt a premonition, she'd never seen Harry like this. Usually they chattered away happily, making small talk if there was nothing more serious to occupy them. But today was different.

'This is to do with you,' he said. 'In fact, this is because of you. I've never met anyone quite like you and you've disturbed my life. There have been times when I've wished I'd never met you.'

'Thank you for that compliment,' she said.

'You know what I mean. When I'm with you, you make me happy. But before I was contented with my life. Now I'm not.'

'Then you'd better change your life.'

'It's not that easy.' They swung across the road, parked in a layby so they could see for miles across the plain below them. But though he appeared to be staring, she knew he was seeing nothing.

In a voice more dull than she'd ever heard from him, he started.

'When you're young, when you're a child, I think you feel more than you do as an adult. Some things seem to be so unfair, so unanswerable. You don't have the maturity to see that there might be another side, another way of looking at things. Anyway...I was an only child. I discovered later that after having me my mother couldn't have more children, some infection in the uterus. Perhaps things might have been different if there'd been more of us. Or perhaps the misery might have been doubled.

'I remember being happy, I was about five. I thought my parents were happy. My mother was a teacher, my father something in local government. We had a nice house in a nice suburb with a nice small car and they took me to Spain every summer but I found it too hot. Like I said, I was happy.

'Then my father was killed in a car crash. Just like that. Apparently no one's fault. The police came round and told us. Everyone was sympathetic, but after a while my mother had to cope as best she could. And she didn't manage very well. Kim, I can imagine, I think, what she had to suffer. I do know what we both had to suffer. And I've thought about it a thousand times. Once she said, ''Why did it have to be him? Why not someone else?'' And I knew she was thinking of me.'

Harry paused again, Kim waited and wondered. Should she sit quietly or comment? His story was so painful that she could share his anguish, feel what telling it was doing to him. Tentatively, she reached over, took his hand. He held her hand tightly, but didn't look at her or give any indication that he knew she'd moved.

'It was odd in our house,' he continued. 'I was fed, clothed, taken to school. But my mother was somewhere else, somewhere on another planet. And I needed comfort!

'Then things apparently got better, at least for her. Three months later my mother took up with another man. He came to live with us. He wasn't unkind to me, he just never liked me. But my mother became besotted with him. In fact, they were besotted with each other. There was no room for me.'

Kim thought. 'Perhaps she was mentally ill,' she suggested. 'The shock must have been catastrophic.'

'I thought of that. It is possible. I can only say that I saw no signs of it then, nor can I recollect any signs of it. But it is possible, even likely. All I can remember is that he was offered a job abroad. And I was put into care.'

Another silence. 'And then you...'

'I was a good, obedient, docile little boy who never caused anyone any trouble. I found out very quickly that you don't really need other people. Other people betray you. But I found solace in work. I was a good student, I had good teachers, they guided me and when I was eighteen I got a place in medical school. I received a letter from my mother shortly afterwards. I tore it up without reading it. End of dreary story.'

Kim stared at him in disbelief. 'You never saw your mother again?'

'She didn't try to get in touch. And neither did I. What was the point? We had nothing to say to each other.'

'And you've never been in touch since? Harry, that's terrible. Have you ever thought, just out of curiosity—?'

'Too late,' he said, guessing what she was going to say. 'She's dead.'

For the moment he didn't seem to want to say more. Kim sat there, grappling with what he had told her, trying to imagine the misery he must have gone through. 'I'm being selfish,' she said. 'I'm thinking about myself. How many people have you told this to?'

'In effect, none. A few people know a few bits. You're the only person I've told the full story to. Well, the only person but one.'

'Why me?'

He looked ill at ease. 'Because…I don't want you to be hurt. Because I thought you, of all people, would understand. I want you to understand me, perhaps even forgive me.' He started the car again, and they drove even higher into the Wolds.

'And you haven't been able to get over it yet? Harry, it must be fifteen years ago!'

'About that. And at one stage I thought I was over it. But then…'

She looked at him, horrified. 'There's more?'

'Yes. And once again I've never told anyone but

you. That is, anyone I care about. You know I like babies?'

'I've seen you in the unit,' she said. 'Of course I know you like babies.' She paused then said, greatly daring, 'You'd be a good father.'

'I was a father once.'

Five stark words. She looked at him in horror.

They came to a village, high on the side of a hill. They passed farm buildings, agricultural wholesalers', a couple of pubs. It was a floral village, everyone seemed to have made an effort to have windowboxes, hanging baskets. There was a green, even a pond with ducks. And next to it there was a church.

He pulled up outside the church. 'St Mary's,' he said, 'perhaps six hundred years old. I picked this place, it puts everything in perspective.'

From the back seat he took a small sheaf of flowers, she hadn't noticed it before. Then he led her into the churchyard. They walked through leaning ancient gravestones to where the later burials were. They saw the odd bunch of bedraggled flowers. And then he stopped.

They had come to a quiet corner set aside, a set of tiny stones in a pleasant little garden. 'This is where they bury cremated children,' he said. He walked over to a small stone, placed the flowers by it. Not knowing what to do or think, Kim looked down at the inscription. *Helen Gregory. 17/7/1999-28/11/1999. Loved and Lost.*

'She didn't live very long,' Kim said, a quaver in her voice. 'Who was she?'

'She was my daughter. But I never saw her, never even knew she was alive…till she was dead.'

Even at that moment she could see his reserve. His face showed no emotion, he just stared bleakly at the little stone.

Not so Kim. She threw her arms round him, wept for him. Then she looked up at that stone-cold face and screamed, 'Harry Black, what's wrong with you? Can't you spare one tear? Just once can't you show some feeling? Harry, she was your daughter!'

'Crying won't bring her back,' he said.

Kim buried her head on his shoulder again and sobbed until she was spent. Then she seized his arm, dragged him to a nearby bench. 'You know why I'm crying?' she gasped. 'Not for your daughter, poor little mite, but for you. There's something inside you that is dead, too. Now, tell me what happened!'

Silently, he passed her a handkerchief. She wiped her eyes, took a deep breath. And after a minute she said, 'I'm better now. Tell me.'

His voice was still calm. How could it be? But it was, and she made herself listen.

'The mother was Pauline Gregory, a nurse in the hospital I was working at. We had what I thought was an amiable relationship. She knew that there was nothing serious, we were just having a good time together.'

'Did this Pauline know your relationship was just amiable, that there was nothing serious?'

He looked at her in surprise. 'Well, I did make it clear to her that that's all it was.'

'Do you think making it clear is quite enough?' Kim asked with a sudden flare of temper. 'Are you

sure you didn't say that just to salve your conscience?'

'Possibly,' he said. 'In fact, she was the only other
person apart from you that I've told about my up-
bringing. However, she did get far too keen. She
started talking about where we were going, what our
relationship meant. She wanted to know what our
future was—when we were going to get married. So
I said I had no plans to get married. And I backed
out of the relationship. We had a big row, she left
the hospital, saying that I cared more for the babies
in my ward than I did for her.'

'The picture,' Kim said. 'That photo in the book
that you tore up.'

He nodded. 'That was Pauline. Gave me a shock
to see her after all this time. Anyway, perhaps she
was right about me caring for the babies. And I heard
nothing from her for a year. Then…then…'

For the first time Kim got some idea of how he
was suffering, what he was truly feeling under that
granite exterior.

'Then I got a letter and a parcel from Pauline. She
said she was going to America, that she would never
come back. After we'd parted she'd found out that
she was pregnant. Since I obviously didn't care for
her, she hadn't let me know. The baby was born
prematurely, at thirty-two weeks. It—she—never really had a chance but she lingered on for four
months. She was kept in hospital all that time.
Pauline just lost interest.'

Kim knew this wasn't exactly rare. Knowing that
their babies stood very little chance of surviving,
some mothers cut themselves off from all emotional

connection with their child. It was brutal but sometimes effective therapy.

'What happened then?' she asked.

'I hadn't realised just how much she hated me. She wrote that, knowing my great love for children, she thought I might like to have my child's ashes. She enclosed the birth and death certificates. And I arranged for Helen to be buried here.'

Kim walked over to the little grave, tears blurring her eyes. Then she went back to him and said, 'You've told me a terrible story, Harry, and you've no idea how I feel for you. But there's still more, isn't there? You're still young, you can cope with tragedy if you try.'

He shrugged. 'I just decided that relationships were not for me. I already felt let down once, by my mother. I tried not to hurt Pauline and what she did to me was brutal and vindictive and cruel. You can't trust women, you can't trust anyone. Kim, I would have loved that child. I would have liked just to have seen her—if only for an hour in hospital. But she's dead. And I visit this grave about twice a month but it doesn't do much good.'

'You've told me this,' she said slowly, 'and I know it must have been hard for you. Thank you so much. I feel I really know you now, and you've no idea how sorry I feel for you. But now I need time to think. Will you drive me home?'

They drove back to her flat in silence. All the way she had been thinking about what she had to say, how to say it. When they drew up outside her door, she leaned over to kiss him. Then she said, 'I'm not giving up on you, Harry Black. You think you can hide behind that cheerful face, being everyone's friend but close to no one. You think you can wander through life, picking up the odd girl here and there for a quick liaison and then part with no harm done. Well, that's not a good way to live. Harry, I'm going to show you that there's more to life.'

'It's been tried before,' he said bleakly.

'You wanted to put me off. You've managed to do just the opposite. Harry, now I…care for you more than ever.'

Harry was always in a sombre mood after he'd visited his daughter's grave, but this time it was much worse. He had felt he had to explain things to Kim. When he'd done so he'd hoped she'd come to understand him. Know why he couldn't commit himself fully to any woman, why he feared any long-lasting relationship. And he'd got it wrong. He should have known how she would react.

Her words echoed in his mind. *I'm going to show you that there's more to life.* No other woman had ever said anything like that to him. And that had been a declaration dragged out. Kim had said it in pain and suffering. But he knew she'd meant what she'd said.

He had driven his car to the entrance to the hospital. There was a roundabout there where he could turn, drive back to her flat. He slowed, thinking, wondering if he should return, tell her that it would be hard but that he would try, that she was the one woman whom he felt he could trust. He remembered the night in his flat.

But then the old bitterness overwhelmed him.

Soon he would be in Australia. It would be a convenient escape. Better for him, better for her if they tried to forget each other, move on to new and separate lives.

But as he drove out of the hospital gates, he knew it would be hard.

CHAPTER FIVE

THE Princess Mary Hospital was at Calthorpe, twelve miles inland from Denham. It was in the process of being closed and all its work was being transferred to the Wolds Hospital. But there were still a few departments operating, and a paediatric outpatients clinic was held there once a week. Travelling long distances with a new baby wasn't a good idea.

Harry was going to take the clinic, Kim was going to observe and perhaps help. This was new work to her, she was looking forward to it.

Harry had offered her a lift to the hospital. She had thought about it for a moment then declined. For one thing, he might have to stay longer at the hospital. It was a fine day, the sun was out, she sang as Bessie chugged steadily along the main road. She felt happy, she was learning a lot. For the moment she wouldn't think about her relationship with Harry, that could come later. She found she could separate her love life from her professional life. For now they enjoyed working together and enjoyed each other's company. And that was all.

She found the clinic. Harry was already sitting at a desk with a great sheaf of files in front of him. 'My favourite SHO,' he said amiably. 'Grab a coffee and then come and help me with these files. And may I say that you look particularly fetching in that pink dress.'

'I'm your only SHO so I have to be favourite,' she pointed out, 'and may I say that you look particularly fetching in that striped shirt.'

'Ironed it myself this morning,' he said proudly. 'Note the beautiful knife-edge creases. We bachelors know how to look after ourselves.'

'Only a man would expect praise for wearing an ironed shirt. Now, what am I doing this morning?'

'Look through these cases. We'll look at the babies and later on you can write up my notes on them and arrange further visits. You can do a few of the tests as well. Now, white coat over there. Let's start.'

He gave her a big cheerful smile and for a moment she found herself thinking how wonderful… No, that kind of thought was banned while they were working.

She quickly found that working a clinic was still fascinating, but not as intense as working on the unit. There wasn't the same underlying tension as there was on the unit. The babies here tended to be thriving, to be getting better. The parents were more easy-going, more inclined to stay for a chat.

'This is George Oliver,' Harry said. 'He's five months old—but if you take off six weeks for arriving prematurely, then he's only three and a half months old. And he's a lovely little lad. He's thriving. No great problems, Mrs Oliver?'

'None at all, doctor. When he was born we worried that…but he's fine now.'

Kim was always interested to see how Harry handled his little charges. There was love in the way he picked them up, stroked them, held them. Harry doted on children. He deserved to have some of his own. Another line of thought that Kim decided she had to ignore.

'This is a very smart coat and hat he's wearing,' Harry went on. 'Did you knit it yourself?'

Mrs Oliver laughed. 'Me? Knit? When would I find time? No, his great-grandmother knitted this. She was a bit upset because it wasn't finished when George here was born.'

'Well, he looks good in it,' said Harry. 'It's a pity I'm going to undress him.'

It was a quick examination and soon Mrs Oliver and George were on their way, contented that all was well.

'I like examinations like that,' said Harry.

The next two or three babies were equally problem-free. Kim sat at a side table, taking notes and arranging follow-up appointments. But then Mrs Kenyon came in and she had a problem. Roy, her baby, whimpered as they talked, even though Mrs Kenyon held him close to her. 'He's got the snuffles, Doctor,' Mrs Kenyon said, 'and he's been hot and off his food a bit. Not drinking very much at all.'

Kim noticed that Harry frowned slightly when he heard this, but he said nothing. He examined the whimpering child as quickly as he could, then asked Kim if she'd like to do the same. She did so. 'What would you suggest, Dr Hunter?' Harry asked.

Both mother and Harry looked at her, and Kim guessed that he had set this up as a test to see how confident she was in making an unaided decision.

'Well, his temperature is a little high,' she said after a moment's thought. 'And not getting enough fluids is a problem, especially in this weather. But I don't think there's too much cause for worry. I don't believe in having babies in hospital unless absolutely necessary. But in this case, perhaps it wouldn't be a bad idea if Roy was kept in hospital for twenty-four hours for observation.'

'Are you happy with that, Mrs Kenyon?' Harry asked.

'Whatever is best. Just so long as he gets better.'

'I agree. I'd like to keep him in, perhaps for only twenty-four hours. Dr Hunter, could you go with Mrs Kenyon and get Roy admitted?'

'Of course. This way, Mrs Kenyon.'

Kim felt mildly pleased as she walked down the corridor. She had got things right.

The rest of the morning was equally interesting. One woman didn't turn up for her eleven o'clock appointment and Harry grunted as he skimmed through her notes. 'She's been late before,' he said, 'and she doesn't live too far away.'

'Perhaps there are family reasons,' said Kim.

They had finished all their cases except this one and in five minutes would close the clinic. Harry had left the room for a minute. Kim was checking through her quickly written notes when an anxious voice said, 'I'm sorry we're late, we had a bit of trouble at home because I couldn't get a babysitter. Can you see my baby now?'

Kim looked up to see a thin, not-too-young woman whose eyes flicked constantly around the room. The weather was still warm, but she was wearing a coat and had a woollen scarf round her neck.

'Mrs Wright? Of course we can see you now. Dr

Black will be back in a moment, but we'll start without him.'

Harry had now started to let her do the initial examinations of the babies. Melanie Wright seemed to be fine. But Kim chatted away to the mother as she had seen Harry do. Harry had told her to talk as much as possible. 'It puts the mothers at ease, makes them less frightened. It calms the babies. And every now and again you hear something that is significant.'

'You just do it because you're interested and you're a nice man,' she had told him. 'Don't give me this nonsense about hearing something significant.'

So Kim chatted to Mrs Wright, and noticed that every now and again she reached up to ease her fingers under the scarf and rub her neck.

'Having two other children, one aged one and one aged two and a half, must be quite a strain,' Kim said, having studied the case notes. 'You and your husband must have your work cut out.'

'My husband!' Mrs Wright looked shocked. 'He doesn't do woman's work. And bringing up babies is woman's work.' She reached for her neck again gently rubbed under the scarf.

'Well, that's one way of looking at it,' Kim said diplomatically. 'Now, Melanie here seems to be just fine.'

There was relief in Mrs Wright's face. 'Oh, good! So I don't need to come here any more?'

'Well, a couple more visits perhaps,' Kim said. She paused, then said, 'Is there anything wrong with your neck?'

'No, no, nothing wrong!'

But Kim had reached up and eased the scarf to one side. What she saw made her wince. Three parallel bruises on the side of the neck. She had seen these before, they were the marks indicating fingers. Mrs Wright had been nearly strangled.

'Who did this to you?'

'I fell against the fridge in the kitchen,' Mrs Wright said, hastily pulling the scarf tight. 'No one did anything to me.'

'Fell against the fridge? A fridge with fingers?'

'He gets angry. He says it's my fault for having babies.'

Kim realised that Harry had just come in and had heard most of the conversation. Now, he said in a gentle voice, 'Could we get you some cream for those bruises, Mrs Wright? And would you like to tell us about them?'

'There's nothing to tell! I fell against the fridge!'

'We are doctors,' Harry went on. 'We might be able to help. Anything you say will be completely confidential, we don't have to make a report or anything.'

'I've said it twice already! There's nothing to tell!' Now there was a touch of hysteria in Mrs Wright's voice.

Harry gazed at her steadily for a moment, then said, 'Of course not. But if you do want to talk to us, we're always ready to help.' He turned. 'Dr Hunter? Do you think you could organise some cream for Mrs Wright?'

But when Kim returned, Mrs Wright and her baby had gone.

'You can't just let her walk out of here,' Kim said angrily to Harry. 'We have to do something.'

Harry sighed. 'We have no option. Was there anything to suggest that the baby had been harmed, badly treated, neglected, in any kind of danger at all?'

'No,' said Kim, 'the baby is fine. But someone has been trying to strangle her mother. And I bet it's her husband! He sounds an evil so-and-so. We have to do something!'

'Kim! We are doctors, not gods. We follow set rules. And in this case, whatever we might think, we can only act if we're asked to by the injured party. Any doubt about the baby and we have powers. But the woman has to take the first step herself—and that means going to the police. We get enough domestic problems without looking for them.'

'So we do nothing?'

She thought she had never seen him so angry. 'There are some problems we just can't take on. Some problems are insoluble. Now forget it. Understand?'

'I understand,' she said. 'I'd better get on with finishing these notes.'

She bent her head over the desk, conscious that he was looking at her. She didn't look up, and after a while he sighed and left the room.

It took her another half hour to finish writing up the notes and the paperwork, and then she went to find him. She was going back to the unit, he had other tasks that afternoon. She was aware that there was a coolness between them—she didn't like it but there was nothing she could do about it.

'I've finished. I'm on my way,' she said.

Harry nodded. 'Hope you enjoyed the session. And the woman—I know it's hard but there are things you just have to accept.'

'Of course,' she said. And thought to herself that he certainly didn't know her very well. She didn't give up easily.

She had memorised Mrs Wright's address, it was in Calthorpe. She wasn't sure what she could do but she had to try to do something. Anyway, doctors were entitled to make home visits, weren't they?

It was a pleasant little house with a perfect front garden. Mrs Wright was working in it. She looked up as she heard Kim's car door slam, looked at her warily. 'What do you want, Doctor?' she asked.

'I thought we might have a little chat,' Kim said, lying happily. 'We like to see the baby in her home, see that everything is all right.' She opened the gate, moved into the garden.

'I told you that everything was fine. I don't want you to—'

'Who's this, then?' It was an angry, unpleasant male voice. Kim looked up and sighed to herself. This man—presumably Mr Wright—was small, much smaller than herself. And she knew this was going to be a problem. With some men it was.

She tried to speak in a placating voice. 'Mr Wright, I'm Dr Hunter. I've just seen your wife and baby and I thought I might make a follow-up visit to see that all was well at home.'

'We don't need a follow-up visit! The midwife's

been round, everyone's been round. All we want is to keep to ourselves!'

He came down the garden path and the closer he got to her the more angry he was. He saw her size, and that appeared to enrage him.

'I let her go to the clinic. That's now finished so you can just clear off.'

'I'm not used to this kind of treatment, Mr Wright.' Kim thought she was doing well, keeping so cool.

Then the man did something which he should have known was unforgivable. She was going. But he took her elbow and tried to force her to walk faster. It wasn't necessary.

What she did next was also unnecessary—and also unforgivable. She shook her arm free and snarled, 'Get off me, little man.' She saw his face whiten in shock.

Then she reached for Mrs Wright's scarf and pulled it from her neck, saw the deep bruises on both sides. 'This is a serious assault,' she said. 'You could go to prison for doing this. You might have inhibited the vagus nerve, that can result in death. We'll be watching you.'

'She fell in the kitchen! Now, you get out of my house or I'll call the police myself!'

'You don't have to put up with this,' Kim said firmly to Mrs Wright. 'But we can't help you if you don't help yourself.' Then, shaking, she went.

She drove a couple of miles, then stopped by the roadside and waited for the shaking to calm down. She realised that she had probably just done something rather stupid.

*   *   *

Kim drove back to the unit and for the rest of the afternoon sat in a corner and worked on forms. There must be more to medicine than the constant filling in of great sheets of paper! Then, at five o'clock, a stern-faced Chris came to see her. 'Will you come to my room, please, Kim?' She didn't like his tone.

Harry was in Chris's room, his face completely unreadable. He nodded at Kim but didn't smile. She didn't like that either. Chris asked her to sit down and then said, 'I've just had a very unpleasant interview with the hospital's chief executive officer. He had had a visit from a Mr Wright, accusing us—or you—of unprofessional behaviour. He said he was on his way to consult his solicitor. I asked Harry here what happened. He was puzzled because he thought he had given you direct instructions not to carry this matter any further. But apparently you knew better. Now, tell me exactly what happened.'

So she told him. And when she had finished talking, Chris said, 'You went and harassed this man in his own front garden.'

'He needed harassing! He tried to strangle his wife!'

Harry said, 'I told you we were doctors, not gods. We don't judge!'

'Perhaps we should judge,' said Kim.

It was Chris who made her realise how wrong she had been. He asked, 'What happens if that man now stops his wife bringing the baby to the clinic? It's happened before and there's not a lot we can do.'

Kim felt sick. 'I hadn't thought of that,' she said. 'I just got angry.'

'I'm angry, too,' said Chris. 'Not because of the

possible complaint—we can easily deal with that—
but because of the woman and the baby.'

There was a silence.

'I can only say that I'm sorry,' she said. 'I should
have known that acting on impulse was not a good
idea. What do I do to put things right?'

'You do nothing. We wait and see what happens
next. I hope I don't have to tell you that there must
be no contact with these people?'

'No need to tell me,' she said.

'Good.' Then Chris smiled and said, 'We all recognise that what you did was from the very best of
motives. So don't worry too much. There have been
much worse things done.'

Kim felt even more sick. 'I'll go and get on with
my work,' she said.

But she just couldn't concentrate. How could she
have been so foolish? Eventually, after making three
mistakes on three consecutive lines, she decided to
give up on the forms. She'd finish them tomorrow.
And in the corridor she met Harry.

'Are we still working together tomorrow at the
pub?' she asked him.

'Of course.'

She felt a fresh rush of anger. 'You're quite happy
about my professional abilities?'

'I always have been happy with your professional
abilities.' He paused a moment, then went on, 'But
I have to tell you that I wasn't very impressed by the
fact that you thought I did nothing for Mrs Wright
because I didn't care. You're not the only person
with feelings, Kim.'

And that hurt more than anything else.

If she'd been that kind of person she might have cried. But she wasn't. She collected a towel and her costume and went to the hospital swimming pool. There she ignored the children being taught how to swim and swam a hard, punishing, splashy crawl for a mile. When she was exhausted she climbed out. In future she decided she would think before she acted. If she remembered in time.

In the middle of next morning she was called again to Chris's office. Harry was there, too, and she wondered if things had got worse overnight. But the atmosphere was considerably different. Both men were smiling, she was offered a seat and given a coffee.

'Glad to see you're both looking so pleased with life,' she said. 'Have you decided to sack me or something?'

'Have a biscuit,' Chris said genially. 'In fact, have two. We wanted to tell you at once, there's been a very happy ending to yesterday's…misunderstanding. And both of us are delighted about it.'

Kim blinked, she was bewildered. Was she hearing right? 'Why the sudden change in attitude?' she asked.

'I've just had a call from Dr Cartright—you don't know her but she's the police surgeon,' Chris said. 'We know her, she's good at her job. Anyway, apparently this morning Mrs Wright went to the police and made a formal complaint about her husband. The police took a statement, asked Dr Cartright to make an examination and she found evidence of long-term abuse. Dr Cartright would like to talk to you later.'

Now Harry joined in. 'Mrs Wright told the police that she'd made a complaint because she'd found someone who was willing to come out and fight for her. You. You're to be congratulated, Kim.'

'So it's a happy ending?' asked Kim.

'Sort of,' said Chris. 'There will, of course, now be no danger of a complaint from Mr Wright. But...'

'But I still was wrong,' Kim said. 'Yes, now I know that. And I can assure you that nothing like that will ever happen again.' She tried to ignore the expressions on the two men's faces.

'Are you still willing to be my gofer?' Harry asked later in the day. 'Remember, I told you about the big darts competition at the Fisherman's Arms? It's tonight.'

'Of course I'll be your gofer. I said so. It's for charity, isn't it?'

He grinned. 'I thought you might want to come just to be with me.'

'Of course. Just you, me and a pub full of darts enthusiasts. I can't think of anything more intimate.'

'Well, I want to buy you at least one drink. To make up for yesterday.'

She shook her head. 'No, Harry. We both know that I handled things wrongly. The fact that they came out right is just luck.'

'So you won't ever again act in that bull-headed fashion?'

She sighed. 'It's a lot to ask,' she said. 'Now, tell me where do I find this Fisherman's Arms?'

*　　*　　*

It felt like just another SHO's job. Kim sat at a table in a small back room, filled in forms and entered figures on a computer. She had never realised that darts was so complex. From time to time she saw Harry. He was doing what he did best—talking to people, making them feel wanted and at home, organising and dealing with the dozen small crises that cropped up.

It was hard to remember that under that urbane, apparently carefree exterior, there was another Harry. A Harry with more weight to carry than anyone realised. But Kim knew, and she wondered just how easy it was for him to pretend to be everybody's friend.

Eventually the competition was over, her job finished. Harry came to her and said, 'There's to be a quick committee meeting. But if you'd like to stay till afterwards, I'll take you somewhere else for a drink.' There was a pause. 'I'd like you to stay,' he added.

'So I'll stay,' she said.

It would be all right if she stayed for the committee meeting. First she was introduced to the landlord of the Fisherman's Arms and his wife. The wife had had a baby looked after in SCBU, and since then neither she nor her husband could do enough for the unit.

Thanks went to the landlord and his wife and all who helped. A lot of money had been raised—but unfortunately not quite enough. They had hoped to order the machine this month—but they would have to wait. A pity.

Kim noticed Harry had his stone face on again. This wasn't like him, but over the past few days she'd noticed it more and more—when he thought people weren't looking. Perhaps he was worrying about going to… Kim shook her head. Harry wouldn't worry about going to Australia. Could he be worrying about what he had told her? She didn't think that very likely either. And now he was putting his hand up.

'Mr Chairman, I've had a phone call from a solicitor. A man—a person—who wishes to remain anonymous has offered us ten thousand pounds.'

Kim felt the excitement that rippled round the meeting. The chairman looked incredulous. 'Ten thousand pounds, Harry? That would more than cover what we need. But are you sure that the money's really there? This could be some idiot's idea of a joke.'

Harry shook his head. 'I'm certain this is a genuine offer. I phoned the solicitor in question, he's obviously seen the letter and he's arranging the transfer. In fact, I'll guarantee the money myself, so we can start on ordering the scanner.'

The chairman was still in doubt. 'If you say so. Who is this person? Why is he so keen to give us the money?'

Harry shrugged. 'The solicitor said that he—or she—wanted absolute anonymity. No thanks, no letter, no personal contact. For what we're getting, I think we can respect that.'

'Right,' said the chairman. 'Well, I'll start arranging things at once. Meeting closed, I think.'

Twenty minutes later Kim was sitting in the garden of the Escott Arms, waiting for Harry to arrive. She had driven home, left the car and walked over. They had agreed to meet here for the drink he had promised her. It had been a full evening, she had enjoyed it but now she was ready for a drink. And there were questions buzzing in her head.

She looked up. Coming towards her was Harry. In front of him was a waiter, carrying a tray with two glasses and...a silver ice bucket? Kim blinked.

The waiter placed the silver container and the two glasses on the table. 'Shall I open it now, sir?'

Harry nodded, and with a flourish the waiter pulled out a dark green bottle from the ice, cut the foil from round the neck and deftly eased out the cork. There was a satisfying pop. The waiter filled the two flute glasses.

'Champagne?' Kim queried as Harry sat by her. 'What are we celebrating?'

'Well, the scanner fund did well tonight. We raised quite a lot of money with the darts competition. I'm very pleased. And I promised you a drink as apology for the matter of Mrs Wright.'

'I don't deserve a drink. We both know that I was wrong. But the big news is the anonymous ten thousand pounds. Are you going to tell me where it came from? You must have some idea.'

He shook his head. 'Perhaps I'll tell you some day. But the person does want to remain anonymous.'

'Do you think I can't be trusted to keep a secret! Harry, after what you've told me?' She thought a moment and then said, 'Did you give the money?'

He laughed—though she felt it was a little hollow. 'No, it certainly wasn't my money.'

She saw the effort he was making to change his

mood and wondered again why he seemed so low. He said, 'I need all the money I've got to buy Australian hats with corks round the brim.'

'I'm sure you'll look good in one,' she said. 'Now, Harry…'

But he was waving at someone who had just entered the garden. 'Look, there's Erica and Matt,' he said. 'I'll ask them to join us, we'll send for another two glasses and we can celebrate together.'

Kim was always pleased to see her two friends from SCBU. But she would have liked Harry to herself for a few more minutes. Still, if Harry wanted more company than just hers…

It was, of course, a pleasant meeting. They chatted, Matt ordered another bottle of wine—red this time— and then, quite early, they left. Harry walked her back to her flat. He had not used his car all evening.

It was dark, still warm. He took her hand, she was happy that he wanted to hold it. And then they were outside her door—again—and she stopped and looked up at him. 'We're here again,' she said, 'saying good night and thank you for a pleasant evening. Though I do feel that I've been cheated out of something.'

'Cheated?' he asked.

'You know we've got some way to go yet. There's something between us that has to be sorted out, has to be agreed. But you're not ready yet. So I'll wait. Now are you going to shake my hand or what?'

'No, I'm going to kiss you good night. And to hell with what it means or what it leads to.'

So he kissed her, and she loved it. But after a while again it was he who broke it off. He eased her from him, held her at arm's length and said, 'We've got some kind of precarious balance between us. We're close but not too close. And this is rocking that balance.'

'You can't balance for the rest of your life. You're going to have to come down on one side or the other.'

'I've balanced so far,' he said. 'Tell me, though, what d'you think my choices are? What sides do I have to choose between?'

'Me or not me,' she said. 'And, Harry, the choice is yours.'

She heard the breath hiss between his teeth. 'Good night, Kim.' And he was gone.

This time she just didn't think. She had enjoyed the kiss and that was it. She wasn't going to plan or worry and ask herself where she was going. She had been kissed and that was all. She went through her usual bedtime routine and fell asleep practically at once. The future would take care of itself. It would have to.

Kim's calmness was greatly different from Harry's troubled mind. He decided to walk home, not take a taxi. First he'd had a busy day at the unit. The darts competition had been fun but he'd had to keep on the alert for the numerous things that could just go wrong. And talking about the ten thousand pounds had drained him.

So what about Kim? He realised he was getting far more...attracted to her than was good for him. More attracted to her than to anyone he could re-member in the past couple of years—no, remember at all. But now was not the time to give way to feelings like this. He had to keep his distance—stay close, but not too close. He had to! This was the way he lived. He coped.

He had talked about balance. At the moment he was more unbalanced than Kim seemed to be. He didn't like it. He liked to be in control.

But, then, he also liked Kim such a lot. She was tipping the balance the wrong way.

CHAPTER SIX

ALMOST always, the work of SCBU started with a difficult birth—often a Caesarean. The SCBU team would wait in a small theatre adjacent to the main theatre. When the baby was brought over to them it became their responsibility. Before that time it was the responsibility of the surgeon performing the Caesarean section.

Kim was there largely to observe—Chris was in charge and he was assisted by Erica. Kim noticed that even though it had been checked once already, Chris quickly looked over the Resuscitaire—the portable machine that would be used to look after the baby until they could get it back to the unit.

The baby was brought over and laid carefully in the Resuscitaire. 'A little girl,' a voice said. 'Very premature. Severe respiratory distress. She's so weak. She's unlikely to live.' As she had been taught, Kim did an Apgar test, looking at the baby's colour, checking heart rate, muscle tone, breathing and stimulus response. Five out of ten was the final score. Not good. The baby felt floppy, her skin had a blue tinge.

Kim watched as Chris and Erica used suction to clear mucus from the baby's airway, then intubated her and saw that she was ventilated, pumping a precisely monitored amount of oxygen into the tiny lungs. After a while the little girl became less blue.

'It's safe to get her to the unit,' Chris said, 'but I suspect we're going to have to work on this one.'

Once there, the baby was weighed, then put into an incubator and connected to the full monitoring system. Now heartbeat, blood pressure, temperature, respiration levels and oxygen saturation could all be seen and assessed. An umbilical access catheter was introduced and the portable X-ray machine used to check that the line and the tube to her lungs were in place. Chris wrote up a prescription for antibiotics and morphine.

'We've done all we can for the time being,' Chris said to Kim. 'Now it's up to this poor little mite to fight her own battle. I've asked for one-hourly observations, but even if there's any sudden change in her condition, there's no other treatment I can think of.'

'Ultimately, we all fight our own battles,' Kim said.

A nurse came into the room. 'The new baby—her father's outside,' she said. 'He wants to know if he can come in.'

'Take him into my room,' Chris said, 'I'll have a word with him first.' He turned to Kim. 'This is the part of my job that I hate most,' he said. 'Telling parents that their child may not survive. And the thing you have to remember is to be sympathetic, but never give false hope.'

Kim shivered. 'Not a part of the job I'm looking forward to.'

'None of us likes it.' He turned to leave the little ward and then turned and said, 'And the person who hates it most, who takes every death as a personal matter, is Harry Black.'

Kim looked at him. 'I can imagine that,' she said. 'Not really hard, is he?'

Chris shrugged. 'It takes us all different ways.'

Chris talked to the father for a while and then brought him into the ward, introducing him as Mr Landis. He was an older man, with a wispy haircut and wearing a long blue mac—even in this heat. It was the SHO's job to take down personal details for the records. Kim explained this to Mr Landis and then said she would do it when he had spent some time with his daughter. He merely nodded acknowledgement.

Parents acted in different ways when faced with the possible death of their child. Some screamed. Perhaps the commonest reaction was to sit and cry silently, sometimes for hours on end. Mr Landis was one of the unusual ones who showed no apparent sign of emotion at all. Kim knew the man was feeling emotion—she could tell that by the rigidity of his body. But his face remained set and he said nothing.

Kim explained the functions of the various sensors, told him what they were trying to do. Mr Landis showed a vague interest. After taking the family details down, Kim asked, 'Have you thought of the baby's name yet, Mr Landis? We like it if we can call her something more than baby Landis.'

'I talked about names with my wife. We've spent a lot of time deciding and we decided on Victoria. Not Vicky. She'll always be Victoria.'

'It's a lovely name,' Kim said, 'Victoria Landis sounds very well.'

Mr Landis looked down at the incubator again for a while and then said, 'This is my wife's third pregnancy, and probably her last. We had to have AIH, you know. The first two times it just didn't work.'

'We'll do whatever we can for Victoria,' Kim said, not sure what was the right thing to say. 'She's getting...getting the best possible care.'

Mr Landis didn't apparently want to talk any more. He stood by the incubator, stared down at his daughter, his expression remote. After a while he said he'd like to go up to see his wife and would return straight afterwards if that was all right. 'Of course,' Kim said.

A few minutes later, Victoria started to fail. Kim looked at the monitor readings, nodded at Erica and fetched Chris. He looked down and sighed. 'Like I said, there's nothing we can do. Let me know when...'

'When she dies?' Kim asked, unable to hide the quaver in her voice.

'We've done all that is humanly possible,' Chris said quietly.

It's just not fair, Kim thought, it's just not fair. This is that man's only chance of a baby—it's just not fair. There was work to do but she just couldn't do it. She stayed by the incubator, staring down.

She didn't hear Harry come in. He touched her on the shoulder, then put an arm round her and led her forcibly away. 'I've made some strong coffee,' he said. 'You're to come and drink it.'

This was someone she could argue with, someone she could get mad at. 'I suppose you're going to tell me that these things happen, that I've got to get used to it,' she snapped. 'Well, I just don't like it.'

Harry walked over to the incubator, looked down for a while and then up at the monitor. 'They do happen but you never get used to it,' he said harshly. 'Now come and drink some coffee, you're doing no good here.'

She was upset. But not so upset that she didn't realise that Harry was suffering, too. So she went to drink coffee.

While they were drinking coffee they were told that Mr Landis had returned and wanted to be with his daughter again. Kim looked at Harry, horrified. 'Are we going to let that man stand there and watch his daughter die?'

'We certainly are!' Harry said forcefully. 'Of course we're going to let him. That child is part of him. He needs to share as much of her tiny life as possible. He'd blame himself if he didn't. But some-one has to tell him that death is now very likely. Then he can make up his own mind. I'll go and tell him now.'

Kim thought she knew him well now, could rec-ognise the small signs that suggested how he was really feeling. 'I'll tell Mr Landis,' she said.

'No, it's my job and I—'

'I can do it, Harry! I can do it as well as you. You're not the only one with feelings, with sensitiv-ity! And for me, not every little girl we lose is called Helen Gregory!'

Then she gasped at the enormity at what she had said. She looked at his pale face and said, 'Oh, Harry, I'm so sorry. I didn't mean that. I—'

Quietly, he said, 'Of course you didn't, I know that. And I don't want to tell Mr Landis. I'd be pleased if you would, Kim.'

So Kim told Mr Landis. The signs weren't good, there was still some hope but he should prepare himself for the worst. And Mr Landis listened to her courteously. He refused the offer of a drink, said that he'd be fine. Then he stood by the foot of the incubator and stared.

Baby Victoria Landis died an hour later.

Mr Landis said he wanted nothing but that he'd like to be alone with his baby for a while. Then he came out of the ward, thanked everyone for what they had done and said he would now go to tell his wife. He'd be in touch about the other details later. His voice was calm, his expression neutral.

Kim watched him walk away and turned to Harry. 'I know he must be shocked but that's just not normal,' she said. 'He showed no feelings whatsoever.'

Harry nodded, brooding. 'It's not a good idea to bottle up emotions,' he said, 'not a good idea at all. You should say or show what you feel.'

'And I suppose you're an expert on that,' she said. 'Everyone knows what you feel.'

It wasn't fair but she was angry and she had to lash out at someone or something.

'I'm not as good at hiding my feelings as you think I am,' he said.

Then he walked away. She looked after him, feeling guilty.

A death. As in any hospital procedure there was a lot of paperwork and it was up to Kim to do most of it. She felt desolate, scratching the words across the forms—name of the deceased? 'Deceased?' Once she'd been just a baby girl. Now she was the deceased.

Harry looked round the door. 'Feeling low?' he asked.

'Of course I'm feeling low.' She held up the sheet of paper. 'Look at this. The life of Victoria Landis. Age at time of death? Approximately five hours.'

He entered the room, kicked the door shut behind him. 'Kim, it's what we do. Just think, next door there's half a dozen babies and they're going to live. Forty years ago, perhaps all but one would have died. We do well here, Kim, keep that in mind.'

She sighed. 'I know you're right, Harry. And I do get a kick out of the work here. It's different and…better than I thought it would be.'

'Good.' He looked at her a moment and then said, 'Are you still determined to be a GP?'

'I am. It's what I've always wanted.' Suddenly she was curious. 'But what led you into working with neonatal babies? What specially attracted you?'

He shrugged. 'For a while I thought I might be a GP, too. The work is valuable, you help deal with an awful lot of misery. But this kind of work is more intense. The highs and lows are greater. We've just had a low, but think of the high you feel when you see a baby leave who you know has survived because of your efforts. And there's another thing. You see the babies for just a short while. Then they're out of your life, whereas if you're a good GP you get to know your patients, sometimes over years.'

She turned to the photograph on the wall, the one

she had seen when she'd first come here. A happy, bubbling baby—helped to live by SCBU. She pointed to it. 'I know what good we do, Harry.'

'I just think you've got it in you to be a good neonatal doctor. Think about it.'

'I will,' she said. And she thought she would. She'd never done so seriously before.

Then, a week later, things really got bad when she found a message on her answering-machine.

'Hi, Kim, this is Robin. How are you? I'm doing fine.'

Hearing his voice gave her a shock. She had spent three years of her life with him—and she could hardly recollect anything about him. He was out of her life, forgotten. She thought that was a bit upsetting. Had her previous life been worth so little? Or was it that her new life offered so much?

'Both of us have had a while to cool down. I think we ought to meet. We can act like reasonable adults now. I'm going to be in Denham tomorrow morning and I'll stay overnight, there are things we have to discuss. The equity in the flat for a start. Of course, it will all be civilised, we don't need to argue. Will you ring me back on my mobile and tell me where and when we can meet?'

Kim sighed. This was just what she didn't need. But she wasn't going to back out of a meeting as if she was scared of Robin. And there *were* things to discuss. She knew she had time off tomorrow evening, so she phoned Robin's number. Fortunately he was out so she left a message. 'Kim here. There's a hotel by the hospital called the Escott Arms. I'll see you there at eight tomorrow night.'

Then, in a thoroughly bad temper, she went to bed.

She was checking some details with Harry the next morning. The paperwork in the unit never seemed to come to an end, and as SHO it was her job to deal with most of it. Of course, it was very important. But it was often very dull.

She had a list of outpatient babies that Harry specially wanted to see and was making sure that he could be free when they came into clinic.

She wasn't officially on duty that evening. But sometimes she was asked if she could stay late or swap a shift. She wanted to make sure that it wouldn't happen tonight.

'I'm not likely to be needed at all this evening?' she asked him.

'No. Somehow the unit will stagger on without you,' Harry said with a grin. 'Any special reason?'

'My ex-boyfriend—well, partner if you like—is coming over to see me. It's a treat I could do without but it has to be done. I'm meeting him at the Escott.'

'But you go to the Escott with me!'

'It's not your own back yard,' she said, irritated. 'It is free to the general public.'

'What does he want? I thought you were finished for good.'

'We are finished but I've got to convince him. He says there are things that need sorting out. I suspect he wants me back. I'm not looking forward to meeting him.'

Harry frowned. 'Will he be awkward?'

Kim thought. 'Not really awkward. He's like one of those octopuses that get hold of a shell and pull at it gently. It's not a hard pull, but after a few hours the little creature inside the shell gets tired of hanging on and opens. And gets eaten. That's Robin's technique. He'll try to wear me down.'

'Will he succeed?'

'No,' Kim said viciously, 'I'll be angry to start with and he'll only make me more angry.'

'Good luck,' said Harry.

Seeing Robin was like looking at a stranger. Kim blinked as he walked towards her, then automatically moved her head as he tried to kiss her. Was this the man she had spent three years of her life with? She must have been mad! And thinking that made her realise just how much her life had changed in the past few weeks.

'I thought we might have dinner,' Robin said, obviously slightly taken aback at not being able to kiss her.

Kim sighed. 'All right,' she said, 'but I do have work to do. I'd like to be away from here quickly.'

'I've already ordered a table,' Robin said.

They were seated, ordered starter and main course at once. When the waiter left, Kim said, 'About this equity. I hear you're still in the flat and—'

He held up his hand. 'Let's leave that till later. I've brought a few things from the flat that you might want. Your things.' He took out an envelope and pushed it across the table.

She opened the envelope, shook it and gazed at the photographs that emerged. With her forefinger she pushed them round, flicked them over. Photographs of her and Robin together. Photographs of places they had been, of them looking festive. After a while she said, 'You keep them. I've got copies of the ones I want to keep. I don't want these.'

'But I brought them specially for you!'

'I still don't want them. They're of the past and I'm looking forward now.'

'Oh.' Robin looked slightly vexed. 'You haven't found another man so soon?'

Even that couldn't stir her. 'Robin, where would I find another man like you? There isn't one.'

As ever, poor Robin was quite unable to cope with irony. He actually thought she meant exactly what she said. 'These are pictures of the good times that we had,' he protested. 'We were happy together. Come on, Kim, tell me that's right. Weren't we happy together?'

She had to be honest. 'There were some good times,' she admitted. 'Some good times.'

'Good. That's a start. Now, what I think is for you to…'

But then their first course was served and the wine waiter arrived with the previously selected and chilled bottle. As so often in the past, she had to watch as Robin scrutinised the label, sniffed the little poured into his glass and then took a sip. The mouthful was duly rolled round his tongue and then, with an expression of great relief, Robin nodded. The wine would do. Kim sighed. This was a performance she had sat through before.

She wanted to eat, not talk, and merely nodded as Robin picked and commented on the cooking. The food made up for the conversation. Then their main courses came. Again she ate happily while this time Robin told her about his plans for his future. Obviously he had decided to keep the serious conversation till later. That suited her. If she had to eat she didn't want to spoil her meal. She nodded some more and paid little attention.

They finished their meal and Robin nodded gravely. 'Not at all bad,' he said. 'Not what one would expect in a backwater like this.'

'The chef trained in one of the great London hotels,' she told him. 'Now, can we get on with business?'

'Yes, of course. Kim, I—'

He reached across the table, took her hand. Smartly she pulled it away. 'We're here to talk,' she said.

'Of course.' He pursed his lips, looked judicious. 'Kim, we've both had time to cool down, to think where our best interests lie. Things were said in the heat of the moment that weren't really meant.'

'They weren't?' Kim asked interestedly. 'I meant what I said.'

But Robin was not going to be stopped. 'I think it better if we get together again,' he said. 'Perhaps just at the weekends to start with. And we can take things from there.'

She blinked. She hadn't expected a direct appeal like this. 'Not a chance,' she told him. 'I'm just not interested.'

'But, darling, let's think of the advantages. We both—'

It was her turn to interrupt. 'Robin, I told you, not a chance.'

Now he was getting angry. 'I came all this way to have this talk with you. It wasn't necessary but I thought…'

'It is necessary. We need to talk about the equity in the flat. I gather you're going to stay there. What are you offering me?'

He looked at her, horrified. 'May I remind you that it was you that moved out?'

'May I remind you that my name is on the deeds? You wanted just your name but my father pointed out that if I paid half then it should be in our joint names. I paid half the deposit, half the bills, half the mortgage. I'm happy for you to stay in the flat and I'll sign over the deed to you. When I've received my money.'

He looked bewildered. 'Kim, I thought we loved each other. Now are we fighting over money?'

'We certainly are,' she said cheerfully.

'This is just not you. I'm going to have to wait a time for you to come to your senses. I know you will in time. When you're ready, phone me and we'll talk. You know in your heart that I'm right.'

'Robin, I—'

'Is this a private fight or can anyone join in?'

Kim looked up, startled. There smiling down at them, a pint of beer in his hand, was Harry.

There was silence for a moment. Then Harry said, 'Aren't you going to introduce me to your friend, Kim?'

It didn't take long after that. It took Robin about five minutes to realise that, in spite of hints and guarded requests, Harry had no intention of moving from their table. Eventually he said, 'Dr Black, this is a private conversation. It's…interesting to meet you but Dr Hunter and I need to sort out assorted personal matters.'

Harry beamed at him. 'I'll happily go,' he said, 'when Kim asks me to.'

'Kim?' Robin asked.

'How much are you prepared to offer me for my share of the equity in the flat?'

Robin just couldn't believe what he was hearing. 'I came here to talk about—'

'I came here to talk about money,' Kim interrupted. 'Nothing else.'

'In that case, I'll leave you here with your…your friend. You have my number. Ring me when you come to your senses. I'll pay the bill on the way out.'

And he left.

Harry and Kim looked at his disappearing back. 'I don't think he likes me very much, does he?' Harry asked her.

She looked at him in exasperation. 'Harry, why did you do that? You're supposed to be Mr Cool, Mr Don't Care. Why did you come here to pick a fight?'

He looked at her thoughtfully. 'I'll be honest with you. I just don't know. I'm well aware that you can look after yourself, you're nobody's pushover. But I had this urge to—'

'To protect the helpless little woman? Harry, you're in a bad way!'

'Yes,' he said after a pause, 'perhaps I am.

Anyway, I've got you to myself now. Does it matter that he's left?'

'Just a bit. We were going to negotiate on the money that he owes me.' She saw the alarm on his face and went on, 'Harry, I'm not bothered about the money, but I'm going to get it because of the principle of the thing. I'm more angry at you thinking that I couldn't cope. I could cope and I did.'

There was a long pause. 'Did you have any pudding?' Harry asked.

'No. And I fancy an ice cream.'

'Then I'll order two sundaes.'

They ate the ice cream in silence and it gave her time to think, to examine exactly what she was feeling. She wasn't angry at Harry—in fact, she rather liked the fact that he'd come charging in to help her. Even though she hadn't needed it. It showed a side of his character she hadn't seen much of before. He knew she could look after herself, but he wanted to help anyway. He cared for her.

She said, 'Harry, this just won't do. You're taking on more than is…than is proper. You're acting like a jealous and protective lover and you aren't one, though I'd like you to be. You've settled that.'

'I know. And I'd be kidding myself if I said it was an accident I was here. I came here to…to spy on you. To make sure that you were all right. And when I saw him trying to persuade you, I was angry.'

She laughed. 'Harry, we can't be nothing to each other. But we've both agreed that we can't be lovers. And I still like your company very much.'

'Of course,' he said. But she thought he wasn't

too happy with the idea. Well, the solution was up to him!

'I do have a legitimate reason for wanting to talk to you,' he said after a while. 'In fact, I've got two. The first is that I'm leaving tomorrow night for a fortnight in Australia. I was going in a few weeks' time, but there's been some staffing difficulties and Chris asked if I could bring my trip forward. It's all been arranged. I'll look at the new job, meet the people I'm going to work with, see about accommodation.'

'I'll miss you,' she said. She felt a pang. He would come back—but shortly after that he would disappear from her life for ever. She had known that before, but now it was becoming a reality she realised she had been half hoping that he'd change his mind. 'What's the other thing you have to tell me?' she asked.

'Not tell, ask. When I get back there's a wedding. An old girlfriend of mine is getting married. I've got an invitation for myself and a guest. I'd like you to come.'

'The wedding of an old girlfriend?'

'Well, we did remain friends. And I know the groom quite well.'

She shook her head. 'Harry Black, you are hopeless. All right, I'd love to come with you. I like weddings. Now, later than I intended, I'd better go home.'

'It's still raining. Shall I drive you home?'

She thought for a moment. 'Yes, I'd like that. Then you can come in for ten minutes, one coffee, one kiss, and if I want more than one kiss you are to say no.'

'Deal,' he said.

'One more thing. I'll drive you to the airport.'

'Now, that I would like. But you take my car—I'm not risking travelling in Bessie.'

'Shame on you,' she said.

He looked round her little flat uneasily, less comfortable than the first time he had visited her. He seemed less certain of himself, and she wondered why. After they'd finished the coffee he said, elaborately casually, 'Robin is quite good-looking.'

'Yes. I suppose that's what attracted me to him in the first place. And it's always nice, being wanted. It took a long time to discover I'd made a massive mistake. And that means that next time I'll be more careful.'

'You and me both,' he said, and she wondered exactly what he meant.

He stood. 'One kiss,' he said.

She stood, too. 'Just one. But for how long?'

It was much, much longer than she had thought and she wanted it to go on for ever. And then it was he who stopped—again.

'I want more. So I'm stopping,' he said. 'Good night, Kim.' And he was gone.

Kim had dealt with this twice before. She did the same again—she blanked off her mind, calmly went through her usual nightly routine and was quickly asleep. She could learn not to feel things, not to yearn after what she couldn't have. It was easy really. Wasn't it?

* * *

Harry drove slowly home, his tyres hissing on the wet roads. He thought about the kiss. He had felt the longing in Kim, knew that if he had kissed her again she would have been unable to resist.

And then things would have progressed. Perhaps they would have ended up sleeping together. He knew that both of them had feelings that were strong enough. And there was nothing he wanted more at this minute than to sleep with Kim.

Then he realised that there was something he wanted more. He wanted permanence. But he'd had the offer of that. And it hadn't worked for him.

It was odd, not having Harry around. Kim felt she was part of the team now, she got on well with Chris and all the other members of staff. But Harry had been the one who had helped her settle in, the one she'd turned to first if she'd had any minor problem.

She carefully finished writing up the last series of notes on baby Collins and then sighed. No, she had to be honest with herself. She missed him because he was Harry. He'd only been gone a week and already she… She had to get on with her work!

Chris came into SCBU, his usually pleasant face set grimly. 'We'll be getting a new baby in half an hour,' he said. 'Mother's going to have an emergency Caesarean as soon as they can get things organised. She's had some kind of an accident, blood pressure has rocketed. You can leave these till later. I'd like you to come up with me and help collect the baby.'

'Some special problem?' Kim asked.

'Not as special as it used to be. Mother's name is Maggie Keen, she's a long-term drug addict. She's

tried but she hasn't managed to give up drugs completely during her pregnancy. She's on methadone.
Claims that she's come here from Leeds to get away
from an abusive relationship. So we're shortly to be
faced with a pre-term infant who will be born an
addict. Poor little devil!'

'I've never seen you so angry,' Kim said. 'You
obviously feel really strongly about it.'

'No matter what their background, no matter what
they feel or how a new child is going to affect them,
most of our mothers do their best for their unborn
child. I can guess how hard it is to give up drugs.
But I think when you're having a baby, you should
try extra hard.'

'Is there anything else I should know?'

'Well, the mother's already been screened for
AIDS and hepatitis B. Fortunately she's free of those.
We're still going to have trouble with the baby be-
cause it'll be born with withdrawal symptoms.'

Then, somehow, he smiled. 'Do I have to tell you
that it's not our place to judge?' he asked. 'That if
the mother comes down to see her baby, she'll be
treated with the same care that all the others get?'

'I've learned my lesson. I might have feelings but
I keep them to myself.'

'Good. Let's go and scrub up.'

Baby Keen was delivered, placed in a Resuscitaire
and rushed down to the unit. He wasn't in a good
way.

'Methadone is the drug prescribed for weaning ad-
dicts off harder drugs such as heroin,' Chris told
Kim. 'It's better for the mother but sadly it's harder

for the baby. This baby's going to have acute with-drawal symptoms. We do what we can, sometimes it doesn't seem a lot.'

Baby Keen was photophobic and had to be screened from the light. As Chris and Kim watched he had a seizure—Kim found it intensely upsetting to see that tiny body writhing in pain. 'Can't we do anything?' she asked.

'We take special care to see he's kept quiet. Noise as well as light distresses him. As you can see, he's suffering from respiratory distress, we can do some-thing about that, too. He'll be very irritable. I want you to check his blood glucose levels and we can try to adjust them. Then…' Chris smiled at Kim. 'What would you prescribe for this irritability?'

'Chlorpromazine,' Kim said promptly. 'Three- or six-hourly intervals. Especially if there are feeding difficulties.'

'Good. Anything else?'

Kim thought. 'We need to make out a sort of score chart to mark off when the symptoms disappear. That way we can measure how well he's progressing.'

'Good. Now, that is obviously an SHO's job, so you start and I'm going for a coffee.'

'It shall be done,' said Kim.

Next day the mother was brought down by wheel-chair to see her baby. Maggie Keen was thin, younger than Kim. Once she had obviously been quite attractive, now her hair was lank, her skin wasted. And she was belligerent. 'I'm the drug addict and I've come to see my baby,' she announced.

The nurse who had wheeled Maggie down was

polite enough, but she was obviously not impressed by Maggie's attitude. Kim sighed, sent the nurse to get a coffee and tried to talk to her patient's mother.

'I'm so sorry, Maggie, but you can't hold your baby yet. He needs absolute rest and quiet. But you can look at him and talk to him and he'll know that you are there.'

So Maggie looked at and talked to her baby, and Kim saw tears running down her cheeks. 'Is he going to live?' she demanded eventually.

A need for caution here. 'He was premature,' Kim said, 'and there have been problems with him being…well, he's had withdrawal symptoms as some drugs pass through the placenta wall. But he seems to be making progress so we're all hopeful.'

Maggie thought about that and understood the unspoken message.

'And I've been told I can't even breast-feed him,' she said quietly, 'because of…of…'

'Breast-feeding is good but it's not absolutely necessary,' said Kim. 'Lots of babies thrive without it.'

She thought she should try to get onto something more constructive. 'Have you thought of a name yet?'

'His father was called Duane. So anything but Duane.'

'I've got a book of babies' names here,' said Kim. 'Glance through it and see if there's anything you fancy.'

So Maggie looked through the book, and when it was time for her to be taken back to her ward she said, 'I like Nathan for a name. What do you think? Nathan Keen?'

'Sounds good,' said Kim. 'It's got a ring to it.'

'It says that Nathan is the Hebrew for gift. Well, he's been given to me and I'm going to look after him.'

'I'm sure you will,' said Kim, and found that she meant what she said.

Harry sat on the edge of the beach, a beer—a tinnie they called them here—in his hand. The sun's setting rays stretched towards him over the sea and the temperature was perfect. This was the life!

From behind him came the smells of the party barbecue. He had marvelled at the speed and efficiency with which his new friends had organised a beachside party. This was just a casual, after-work, early evening affair. He had been told when he'd arrived that there would be a lot of them.

He knew he was going to fit in. He liked the staff of the department—they were the ones who had invited him to this barbecue. He had seen the laboratory he would be working in and the facilities were wonderful. He had been shown a flat—far more comfortable than his little place in Denham. This job had everything. So why was he not entirely happy? Why was there a feeling that something was missing? Perhaps he was still jet-lagged.

'Not feeling homesick, are you, Harry? You're sitting here looking very thoughtful.'

Natalie came and sat by him. Natalie was another research student as he would be. She had her own project but was in the same lab.

'Just admiring the view,' he said. 'This is fantastic.'

'Laid it on specially for you. We want you to feel welcome.' Natalie drank from her own tinnie. 'I'm looking forward to working with you.'

Something about the way she said it made Harry look at her. She was quite something, he thought. A skimpy bathing costume, a tan, a very attractive smile.

'We'll be working together a lot?'

'And playing together. Here we work hard, play hard. Like I said, I'm looking forward to it.'

Harry pondered that. 'I'm going to start a whole new life, aren't I?'

'Certainly hope so. Don't forget, this is the new world.'

They looked at each other in silence. Then there was a yell from behind them. 'They're ready! Come and eat.'

'I'm going to feed my face yet again,' said Harry. 'Fetch you a steak sandwich?'

'I'll come and eat with you and the gang.'

So they ate and drank and talked, and Harry answered questions on how medicine was in England, how things were different. And soon it was dusk. This was a midweek party, it was to finish early.

Natalie said, 'I volunteered to drive you back to your hotel. But if you want, you can come back to my place. We'll have another beer, we can talk about this work we're going to do together.'

'Talk about work?'

She smiled at him. 'Work or whatever.'

He was really tempted. Natalie was attractive, intelligent. They shared a sense of humour, had things in common. But…he didn't want to start anything. Perhaps he didn't want anyone to get hurt.

'I think I'd better get back to the hotel,' he said. 'I think I'm still a bit jet-lagged.'

She smiled again. 'Can't blame a girl for trying,' she said. 'Shall we get in the car?'

Harry thought that Australia might be a great place to live. But, then…

It was six in the morning. Kim's phone rang. She struggled out of bed. This just wasn't fair. She wasn't due in the unit for a while yet and… But perhaps there was an emergency. She picked up the receiver. 'Kim Hunter here,' she said, still half asleep.

A voice said, 'It's warm here, I've just been for a swim in the sea. We've had a barbecue and I've eaten two steak sandwiches and drunk some very good chilled beer.'

'Harry!' Her heart leapt at the sound of his voice. All those miles away and yet he sounded so close. But she mustn't get too excited. Or, rather, she mustn't show him that she was.

Trying to sound annoyed, she said, 'D'you know what time it is here? You may be having the time of your life but I need my beauty sleep.'

'Now I know what I'm missing. Everyone here is too nice to me. I need to be shouted at, and who better at it than you?'

'I'll shout at you. I was having a beautiful dream.'

'About me?'

'No. About someone handsome and considerate who didn't wake people in the small hours.'

There was something she needed to know, but she

didn't know how to ask. In fact, she wasn't quite
sure what it was that she needed. 'What's it…what's
it like out there, Harry? You enjoying it?'

His voice was a little more sober now. 'Well, I
suspect I'm still a bit jet-lagged, even after a week.
But everything here is good. As someone just said to
me, they work hard, play hard here.'

'So you'll be happy there?' She had wondered—
Actually she had hoped, she realised, that he might
not be too keen when he finally got to Australia.

'If you can't be happy here, I don't think you can
be happy anywhere,' he said obliquely. 'Are you
missing me?'

'We're all missing you,' she said. She didn't want
to make a personal declaration. 'I've got the time of
your plane back, I'll meet you at the airport. And
now I'm going to have another hour's sleep. Good
morning, Harry!'

'Good night, Kim,' he said.

She got into bed but, in fact, she didn't sleep—
not straight away. She lay there, warm, comfortable,
thinking of Harry. Exactly why had he phoned her?
she asked herself. He'd be home in a week. But she
was glad he had phoned. It made her feel, well,
missed.

She was conscious of the feel of her cotton night-
dress on her breasts, the slight coolness from her
opened window. It would be so good to… But then
she slept.

CHAPTER SEVEN

'EXACTLY why are you taking me to this wedding?' she demanded. 'We're not a couple, you could have gone on your own. You say the bride is an ex-girlfriend. Why has she invited you? I would have thought you'd be the last person she'd want there.'

'I want to take you so I can reassure the bride that I will not be pining after her for the rest of her life. You will be the most beautiful woman there—except for the bride, of course. The bride is always the most beautiful woman on her wedding day.'

'Yes, I've been told that,' Kim said. 'Why are you suddenly such an expert on brides?'

'It was part of my medical training. And we're going to the wedding because Jenny and I were very close once. But not too close. Then she was spirited away by one of my friends.'

'Close but not too close,' said Kim. 'Where have I heard that before?'

'Well, I like weddings,' Harry went on, unperturbed. 'You'll like Jenny. And you'll like Michael. They'll be a fine couple. He's the local GP, she's a nurse. Incidentally, I do like your outfit.'

'Thank you, kind sir,' she said. 'Weddings are the only occasion I get to wear a hat, and I love wearing hats.'

She was dressed in a newly purchased grey silk suit. There was a long jacket that reached her hips, and under it a sleeveless dress that would be ideal for dancing in. And to top it all, a shamelessly extravagant, broad-brimmed scarlet hat, now resting on the back seat of Harry's car. Though she thought it herself, she did look quite nice.

Bessie had been left at home, they were travelling in Harry's car. She had offered to drive again. She wondered if he was still a bit jet-lagged.

Two days ago she had picked him up from the airport. He had been bleary-eyed and not making too much sense. She couldn't disguise—from herself at least—just how happy she was to see him again.

She had hugged him, he had hugged her back. He'd said he'd missed her and she'd thought there was honesty in his voice. But things were not quite as they had been. He seemed to have changed a little, his voice sounded more…resigned?

'D'you like my new necklace?' she asked. She knew it looked well on her, especially against her tanned skin.

'I like it no end,' he said.

The necklace was made of opals. He had given it to her at the airport, said the stones weren't unlucky and it wasn't anything personal, just a small gift for taking him to and from the airport.

'Harry Black, give a girl a personal present! The very idea!' she had mocked him.

But now he grinned at her and said, 'I had some help in picking that necklace. A girl called Natalie, who I'm going to work with. She invited me to her house one night but I turned her down.'

Kim shook her head in mock amazement. 'That's

just not you. What happened to Harry Black, every girl's friend? I hope you recover soon.'

'Well, as a matter of fact...'

Kim sensed that Harry wanted some kind of a semi-serious conversation about Natalie, but at the moment that was just what Kim didn't want. They were going to a wedding together. They would be as happy as all the other guests. Serious conversations could wait.

They breasted a hill. She looked out of the window and quite genuinely gasped, 'Isn't this just something gorgeous? It's like a fairy-tale village.'

They were high on the moors, still purple with heather. And below them in the next valley was the village, complete with church, green and rows of grey stone cottages.

'It is gorgeous,' Harry said drily. 'And it's where we're going. I hope this fairy tale has a happy ending.'

Kim wasn't going to be put off by him. And it *was* a fairy-tale wedding. It was held in the village church, presided over by a beaming vicar who made it clear that he personally knew the bride and groom. And then—something that Kim had never seen before in England—as the celebratory church bells boomed out, the bride, groom and all the wedding party walked from the church to the reception. In fact, it wasn't too hard as the reception was being held in the grounds of the old rectory which was the groom's home. A marquee had been erected there.

Kim took Harry's arm and they joined the procession of wedding guests.

'I thought that was really lovely,' she said, and added, teasing, 'Did it make you feel like getting married, Harry?'

'Not at all. And I'm glad it's not raining, otherwise this would have been a fiasco.'

She looked at him, concerned. 'Are you really not enjoying yourself?'

'I like both bride and groom and I very much want them both to be happy. But the trouble with marriages is that one in every three ends in divorce.'

'You're an old cynic. That leaves two out of three that are happy. Anyway, isn't within a marriage the best way to bring up children?'

'Sometimes,' he said, and she wondered at the blackness in his face.

But then he became his old cheerful self again. They went into the marquee, ate, listened to the speeches, drank champagne and joined in the toasts. Then they wandered round the garden while the catering staff cleared the floor and prepared the marquee for dancing. Later it was back to the marquee where they found a table on the edge of the floor.

'I'm going to need somewhere to sit down and recover,' Harry muttered. 'I've danced with you before. It's exhausting.'

'You love it as much as I do,' she said. 'Now, come on, the groom and the bride have done their circuit of the floor. We can all dance now.' So they danced.

Later on, the bride and groom walked round the floor, sitting at each table for a while. Kim was introduced, then Harry kissed the bride and shook hands with the groom. The groom grinned and said that the best thing Harry had ever done had been to introduce him to Jenny. Then the bride said, 'I've had my eye on you two. You're an item, aren't you?'

'As all the celebrities say,' Harry said, 'we are only good friends.'

'You can't fool me Harry Black, I know you.'

Jenny moved over to kiss Kim and said, 'He's quite nice really. Not as cynical as he pretends.'

'I'll believe you,' Kim said. 'Thousands wouldn't.'

When the bride and groom had moved on to the next table Kim turned to Harry and said, 'She's lovely, isn't she? Not just to look at, she's lovely to be with. How could you bear to give her up?'

'I know she's lovely. I gave her up because we were getting too close. And there was Mike, chasing her like mad.'

Kim thought about that and couldn't make much sense of it.

She took out her pocket mirror, looked in it and winced. 'The trouble with dancing is that it makes my nose shiny,' she said. 'I need to make some cosmetic repairs. Back in five minutes.'

'I think you're fine as you are,' Harry said, 'nose shining or not. But off you go.'

Kim followed the signs posted on the outside of the house and found the bathroom. And when she came out she found Jenny waiting for her.

Jenny took her arm and led her up a corridor. 'The only way I can get rid of my new husband is to pretend to go to the loo. I've been watching and waiting for you to go. Come in here and we can have a five-minute chat.'

She took Kim into a study and carefully closed the door. 'I'm so happy that I think I can solve everyone's problems,' she said. 'So I'm going to do something really foolish and interfere. You do care for Harry, don't you? Love him even?'

'Love him?' asked Kim. 'He won't stand still for long enough to be loved. In fact, I'm trying hard not to love him. But I don't think I can do it.'

'I know the feeling. All I want to say is…that if I hadn't married my wonderful Michael, I'd have been chasing Harry. He's got a problem, Kim, but I never found out what it was. You know this cheerful, everyone's-my-friend attitude is just a front, don't you?'

'Oh, yes. I know that. But I can't get at what's behind.'

'I know the feeling. But keep trying and don't take too long. If he thinks you're getting too serious, if he thinks he's in danger of hurting you, he'll just up and wander off into the night with that amiable smile.'

'Is that what happened to you?'

'We'd both better get back,' Jenny said without answering. 'Getting married is hard work. But I'd like to do a bit to make Harry happy. For a while he made me happy. So grab him if you can!'

Kim went back to Harry. They danced, chatted to people and Kim felt very much at ease in Harry's company. Then they saw the bride and groom off on their honeymoon. Some guests intended to stay and dance all evening but Kim and Harry decided to go. They'd had a good time—but the party was now over.

'Neither of us is on until tomorrow afternoon,' Kim pointed out when they were near Denham. 'Would you like to come back to my place for a drink? I've got a bottle of champagne, I bought it to celebrate when I left Robin and then decided he wasn't worth wasting the bottle on.'

Knowing she was going to drive home, Kim had had little to drink at the wedding, and Harry had said he would hold back, too. But now there was no need. 'You can walk home afterwards,' she said.

'All right,' he said after a moment. 'That sounds like a great idea. And I do fancy another drink.'

So they went to her flat and she put the bottle in the freezer for a while. 'You sit and read a magazine,' she said. 'There's a copy of *The Lancet* there. I'm feeling a bit sticky, so I'm going to have a shower and change.'

Harry looked at her broodingly. 'I'm feeling sticky myself. Why can't men go to weddings half-dressed like you are?'

She laughed. 'I wouldn't want you to be uncomfortable. But I'm a big girl. If you want, you can shower after me and then borrow my wrap.'

As she said this she felt her heart thumping, felt the tickle of sensation round the edge of her hair. It was an offer she hadn't intended to make. Somehow it had just come out, forced from the depth of her unconscious mind. But now she'd said it she knew it was what she wanted.

'That would be very nice,' he said levelly.

She showered, put on fresh dainty underwear and then a tracksuit. 'Change in my bedroom if you want,' she said as she entered the living room. 'The wrap's behind the door.' She knew her voice was higher than normal. Even to herself it sounded squeaky.

'All right.' Still that level, noncommittal voice. She wondered if he was as nervous as she was.

He came back into her living room a little later. His hair was still wet, slicked down. The wrap didn't look quite as ridiculous on him as it might have done. It was an adventurous purchase of a few months back, when she had wanted to splash out on herself just a little. It was long, in dark red silk with a Chinese dragon on the back. She had deliberately bought too large—so now it just fitted Harry. But the fine material clung to his body, showing the curves of muscle on arms, legs, torso.

'I got the champagne out the freezer,' she croaked. 'It's cold enough now. Will you open it?'

So he popped the cork and filled two glasses. 'We've drunk the health of the newly married couple,' he said. 'Who shall we toast now?'

She leaned forward to clink glasses. 'To the future,' she said.

'The future.' He sipped from his glass, stared at her.

They both finished their drinks without further conversation. Then she put down her glass, walked over to him, put her arms round his neck and kissed him. Hard. She felt his movement of initial shock, then the surge of delight as he wrapped his arms round her, pulled her close to him. And after a wonderful minute—or ten—she made herself break away. When she saw the sadness, the longing in his eyes, it was hard for her. But it was something she had to do. She went back to her seat.

'That was unexpected—and very pleasant indeed,' he said.

'True. Harry, just after we first met we agreed not to get too close to each other. The first reason was that you were going away and I was fed up with men. But that doesn't count now. I have got close to you, closer than I intended. What I need to know is have you...are you closer to me?'

'Close enough to borrow your wrap.'

'Harry! Be serious! This is hard for me so give me an honest answer without any smart-Alec remarks.'

'I wouldn't consciously hurt you for anything,' he muttered. 'You mean...you mean...an awful lot more to me than I have ever anticipated. More than anyone since...'

She guessed. 'Since your mother?'

'Since my now dead mother.'

It was the way he said it that gave her a clue. 'She's only just dead, isn't she? Was that the phone message that you got a month ago? The one you claimed was nothing important but still seemed to upset you?'

'I'm a poor liar, aren't I?' he said with a feeble grin.

But Kim was thinking now, putting things together. 'The ten thousand pounds for the scanner. You said it wasn't your money—but it was left to you, wasn't it?'

'I don't want her money! I want to forget her. There's more money but I'll get rid of it somehow.'

'She only left you money?'

'There's a box of personal papers. When we have probate I'll write to the solicitor and tell him to burn them. She has nothing that I want.'

'That's terrible!' Kim sat and thought. 'You hate her so much you won't take her money?'

'It's not the money, it's the memories,' he said. 'But I'm contented now. The only lesson I've learned from her is to take what happiness I can but make sure that I hurt no one.'

He was sitting there in her wrap. On many men it would have looked ridiculous. But it seemed to suit him, his masculinity emphasised by the softness of the silk, the way it clung to him.

'Take what happiness we can,' she said. 'Well, that will suit me, too. It's getting late. You know you're not going home, don't you? You know you're going to spend the night with me? If you want to, that is.'

Had she said that? The words seemed to hang between them, a fragile bond that he could cut so easily if he wished.

'I do want to,' he said. His voice sounded strained, as if he wasn't quite sure of what he needed to say. 'I do so much want to…but I know just how much it would mean to you, and I don't want to hurt you.'

'There'll be no hurt,' she said, knowing that she was lying. 'And this conversation is getting too deep, too serious. Harry, don't you want me?'

That was enough. He stood, came over to her, and when she saw the depth of desire in his eyes she felt a tiny thrill of excitement, almost of fear. And when he kissed her, his very delicacy made her more aware of the strength of feeling that smouldered underneath.

She was still sitting, he was bent over her. His hands were on each side of her and the only part of his body that touched hers was his lips. And the touch was so delicate.

But she wanted more of him. She reached out, felt for the neck of the gown, pulled it open slightly and laid her hands on his chest. There was the slight roughness of hair, the warmth of his body, and under her fingertips she could detect the thudding of his heart.

Then he stood, eased her up with him, without breaking the contact they had with each other. Then they were pressed together and the kiss deepened into something altogether more serious. She felt that she knew his entire body, the thinness of the wrap doing nothing to hide his obvious growing need of her.

Then she gasped involuntarily. He wrapped his arms round her knees and shoulders, swept her up and carried her through to her bedroom. She marvelled at his strength, she wasn't exactly small.

He lowered her onto her bed. Then he lay half on top of her and kissed her again, a kiss neither searching nor demanding, but underneath she could feel the desperation in him. And then when the kiss ended, she stroked his back and told him to lie there. There were things she had to do.

'You will come back?' There was anxiety in his voice, although he knew she would return.

It was good to be wanted. 'I'll come back,' she said.

It was nearly dark outside now and she closed the

curtains. From the top drawer of her dressing-table she took out four thin candles, arranged them on a glass tray and lit them. She had always loved candlelight. And the room filled with the scent of lavender.

She could see his face, half in light, half in shadow, his expression intent, and she thought her longing for him had never been greater. She stood in the soft light, crossed her arms and made to pull her tracksuit top over her head.

'I want to undress you!' His voice was thick.

But she wanted to tease him. 'No. Lie there. I'm looking at you and I want you to look at me.'

'So long as you come to me soon.'

Then, for a moment, she felt nervous. She wondered what she was doing, why she was being so wanton with a man who had made it clear that he wanted nothing permanent with her, who would walk out of her life in a few weeks. And then she decided she didn't care. She wanted to give herself and care nothing for the consequences.

Consequences? With a touch of doctor's practicality she mumbled that she wouldn't be a minute and fled to the bathroom. The last thing she needed was a baby.

When she returned, she lay by his side on her narrow bed. She hadn't realised that there was so much of her to kiss, so many places where the touch of his lips and his tongue could make her smile or laugh or gasp with pleasure.

And she took pleasure in his body, too, kissing or sliding her hands across the firmness of bone and muscle. They were together and happy, there was no urgency, it was as good to give pleasure as it was to receive it.

But then things changed. She clung to him harder, felt his growing need for her was matched only by her own. 'Now,' she heard herself pleading. 'Please, now, Harry.'

'Yes, now,' he repeated, his voice harsh with desire. And then he was over her, and she took him into her, calling out with the delight of it.

It wasn't long then. There was a pent-up force in both of them that needed speedy release. Moments later there was a joint cry of passion, of culmination.

'Kim, I...' he said after a while, but she put her hand over his mouth.

'No talking tonight,' she said.

So he kissed her for a while and then they both slept.

Next morning, she woke early, slipped out of bed and made two mugs of tea. Then she came back to bed, pressed her warm body against his. She wrapped her arms round him, explored his body. Then she giggled and whispered, 'Harry Black, I know exactly what you're thinking.'

This time things were over even more quickly— but were no less delightful.

'Not even time for the tea to go cold,' he told her, and she pinched him.

He insisted that she lie in bed while he made breakfast. Then he suggested that they go for a walk. 'We need to work off all that food and that champagne,' he told her.

So they went first to his flat where he changed.

Kim looked at the boxes, some already packed and sealed, but decided to say nothing. Then he drove her out to the clifftop.

She was happy just to be with him and to be out in the sun walking with him. 'This is not like you, you're quieter than I've ever known you,' he gently teased her as they stared over the cliff at the white sails of the yachts in the distance.

'I'm happy. But over the past twenty-four hours we've had so much excitement that I feel that we both need a bit of quiet, a bit of just being. It's good just to be with you, Harry. I feel contented.'

'I know what you mean. But things have changed. We'll have to talk about them at some time.'

'I suppose so.' She thought for a moment and then said, 'But have you noticed that we tend to be happier when we're doing, not talking?'

'Depends on what we're doing,' he said, and ducked when she tried to hit him.

After a while he took her hand and pulled her off the path, took her to a sheltered spot where they could sit and listen to the roar and hiss of the waves on the beach far below.

'Harry, last night. I think that now I've got to say something about it.'

'Last night, this morning, both were wonderful,' he said. 'Something I doubt I'll ever forget.'

'Nor me. But we were both excited after the wedding, there was the champagne and everything, perhaps we were not both fully in control. What I want to say is, you're not to feel committed to anything.'

'So you're not going to make me marry you?' he asked with a grin.

'Well, not yet. In fact, not at all. But you know what I mean. We're as we were before.'

'Exactly as before?'

'Exactly as before,' she said firmly. She thought this was his chance to say something different, to tell her that things had indeed changed. But he didn't take that chance.

'OK, then. Let's just see how things go for a while.'

'We'll do that. We're both free agents,' she managed to say in a cheerful, light-hearted tone. But she didn't believe a word of it, and when he didn't contradict her she could hardly cope with the misery. But this was the course she had to follow. No way would she pressurise him. He had to change his mind on his own account. But perhaps she could encourage him a little.

She found a chance three days later. They were walking through the hospital grounds and had stopped to look at squirrels running up and down an old beech tree.

'I think you owe me,' she told him. 'I think I'm entitled to something from you and I want it now.'

As ever, his face was placid. 'Whatever you want you may have,' he told her. 'I know you now. I can't think of anything you might ask that I won't give.'

'I want to talk about Pauline Gregory.'

His face blackened. 'There's nothing to talk about. I told you the facts and I want nothing more to do with her.'

Kim felt herself struggling. 'I want to help you, Harry. You feel that she betrayed you in the worst possible way. And I agree. What she did was terrible, appalling. I can feel your hurt, but I just want you to try to think what she must have suffered.'

'I suffered enough for both of us.'

'Did you? Did you have a child, go through the pain, feel that disappointment? Remember, having an ill premature baby is more than a tragedy, it's a disappointment. Did you feel that on your own?'

'She only had to ask! I would have helped.'

'Did she know that? If you had been rejected as she felt she had, would you have asked for help?'

Kim would have preferred him to get angry. It was hard when he became cold and logical. 'She knew me well enough. Certainly I have faults but I like to think that I also have strengths. Kim, in a similar situation, would you have come to me for help?'

She knew he was watching her, waiting for her answer. 'Nothing would make me act with the cruelty with which she dealt with you when she sent you the ashes. But you have to understand that that cruelty might have been the act of a distraught mother. Someone who felt betrayed.'

'She had no right to feel betrayed.'

'We're talking emotions here. Not rights.'

'Are you taking her part, saying that I—'

'I'm taking nobody's part! I'm trying to feel my way into a mother who, rightly or wrongly, feels she's been let down, who has lost her baby and who wants to fight back.'

He was cold again. 'So what do you expect of me?'

'I expect nothing. It would be nice if you could think and perhaps realise that she wasn't completely evil. You lost a child, Harry. So did she. Who hurt most?'

He stood silent for a while. Then he said, 'I'll think about that. Now, can we continue our walk?'

'You're not mad at me?'

'No. Perhaps I'm a bit mad at myself. Walk?'

Kim had a hard afternoon on the unit. Maggie Keen, the drug-addicted mother, came in to see her baby. She appeared to be sticking to her detox programme, but she was finding it hard and wanted to take out her anger and her misery on anyone who was handy.

'I didn't like the way Nurse High-and-Mighty looked at me,' she said to Kim. 'I'm not dirt, you know.'

'She only asked you not to touch the incubator,' Kim said wearily. 'We go to a lot of trouble to keep it sterile, we only want the best for our babies.'

'Just so long as my baby gets as good attention as any of the others.'

'He will. You know he will.'

Then Maggie had one of her lightning changes of mood and burst into tears, saying that she wasn't good enough to be a mother and that everyone was lovely to her.

'Just keep trying,' Kim said. 'You'll get there in the end.' And after a while Maggie cheered up a little, accepted a coffee and smiled at baby Nathan again. Then she left after taking up an hour of Kim's time.

Kim knew that Maggie was having a rough time, that drug withdrawal was hard, that she was suffering more than anyone could imagine, that she wasn't really sure what she was saying. But she should try to remember that there were other people on the planet.

When Maggie had gone there was more paperwork to wade through. She made herself a cup of strong coffee to try and stimulate her jaded spirits—and promptly spilled it over the past half-hour's work. No way of drying it, it would all have to be written out again. Then some sheets went mysteriously missing—and when she found them she realised it was her fault that they had been misplaced. That made her angrier than ever. Altogether, not a good shift.

There was no sign of Harry, he must be working on one of the regular paediatric wards. But he usually dropped in, just to say hello. She went home in a temper.

Next day was just as bad. The work was boring, nothing of interest happened. And there was no Harry to cheer her up, to make some smart remark that would make an otherwise bleak day seem interesting. She realised that he was avoiding her on purpose. Slowly she was coming to the conclusion that by bringing up the subject of Pauline she had possibly ruined what little they had. And it wasn't fair! She felt lower than ever.

CHAPTER EIGHT

IT WAS the first of October, and Kim was working in the ward when Harry came in. 'I've handed in my notice,' he told Kim. 'I've just been to tell Chris officially. I leave at the end of December.'

'I hope you'll be happy in Australia,' she said flatly. 'I'll be sorry to see you go, you've been a good medical teacher to me.'

'I'll be happy,' he said.

But she thought he said it with too much conviction. Perhaps he was having the odd doubt. She said, 'I know you've always said that—'

The door burst open, Erica was there. 'Nathan Keen's arrested,' she gasped.

Instantly Harry was out of the room, half running to Nathan. Kim followed at once, listening as Erica briefed Harry.

'Difficulty breathing, fractious, but he's always been like that. Then his temperature spiked, and oxygen saturation levels dropped, he went pale, blue lips. I was just coming for you when he arrested. So glad you're on the ward!'

'Oxygen and CPR,' Harry said calmly. 'We'll ventilate him. I want bloods checked a.s.a.p. But first…'

He put his hand through one of the portholes on the incubator, felt for Nathan's chest. Then, very delicately, he pressed rhythmically. Cardiac massage, Kim thought.

But it worked. The little heart started to beat again, the vital signs on the monitor slowly returned to—well, near normal. The extra oxygen had its effect.

The bloods were taken, sent for instant analysis, the portable X-ray machine brought in. Harry scowled when he saw the white patch on Nathan's chest. 'Sepsis, I'll bet,' he growled. 'I wonder where he picked that up.'

Then he remembered that he was a teacher. 'So what do we do, Kim?'

'After we've seen the blood results we prescribe antibiotics.'

'Good. But for now we wait and watch.'

It was an hour before he could be persuaded to move from Nathan's side.

Later that afternoon they sat in the doctors' room and drank coffee. Saving Nathan's life had brought them together and if only for a while, there was an intimacy between them that both could recognise. She felt she could question him.

'When you thought that you'd won,' she said, 'when you decided that Nathan was out of danger, if only for a while, you smiled. You looked as if you'd won the lottery. Now I know why you're a paediatrician. You love kids, don't you?'

'You're no good as a paediatrician if you don't love kids. It should be part of the job description.'

'But it's a bit extra-special for you. Why?'

'I really like working with neonates,' he said, 'and prems especially. Those who don't seem to have a chance. They remind me…'

She thought she caught something in his voice. He

was tired, had let something slip, had meant to say something more then had broken off. 'Remind you of Helen?' she asked gently.

The room became suddenly still. It was as if they were insulated from the noise outside, living in a place where only the two of them mattered. She wondered if finally she had gone too far, pressed him again to see things that he wished to keep hidden. Then he said, 'No. They remind me of lots of hours working in the past. Any more coffee?'

Silently she passed him her cup, equally silently he filled it for her. Then he said, 'You're right, of course, they do remind me of my daughter. Do you know that you're the only person ever to say that to me? The only person ever to know me well enough to say it to me?'

'I'm glad that you told me about Helen. I'd like to think that it's something that we can…share?'

'You…you never knew her. How can you share in my grief?'

'Harry, I can share in any of your feelings that you'll reveal to me. And I want to share, because I…care about you.'

She crashed her coffee-cup down onto the table. 'We—you—have just saved the life of little Nathan. His mother is a drug addict, which is bad enough. But perhaps what is worse is that she's alone. There's no partner she can turn to for comfort, no one she can lean on, no one who can feel for her. And that's hard. If you can share your misery then it's halved. You know, there was a song I dimly remember from my youth. And it had some line about people who need people are the luckiest people in the world. You want to think about that, Harry.'

He didn't get angry. He looked puzzled, rubbed his face. Twice she thought that he was going to speak but then he stopped and thought some more. Finally he said, 'Perhaps…' But a nurse came into the room, wanting a bit of advice. And there was no chance for any further intimate conversation.

There was no chance to carry on with the conversation, though Kim desperately wanted to. Still, slowly they got back together again. There was the same co-operation at work, the same intuitive knowledge of what the other was about to do. Working with Harry was marvellous. And if they weren't lovers, well, it was up to him to take the next step.

It seemed odd to use her hard-learned computer skills to help run a darts competition. The idea had been that being computer-literate would help her practise medicine. But the darts competition produced money and the money would produce a scanner. So when Harry asked her if she'd act as his gofer again, she agreed at once.

Then she had to admit to herself that her primary reason for agreeing was to be with Harry.

She did the same work as the last time. The evening was a success. And afterwards the chairman of the committee made a speech thanking people for attending and telling them how well the fund was doing. After the thanks he said, 'And I have more good news. You all know that at our last meeting we were told of an anonymous gift of ten thousand pounds. Well, that money has come through. We have enough for the scanner and it's been ordered. And with the ten thousand pounds came a letter saying that if we raise another five thousand pounds towards any other item of equipment that the paediatric department needs, our mysterious benefactor will send a further five thousand pounds.'

There was a roar of applause. The chairman continued, 'We have no idea who this man or woman is. But if you're listening, a big thank you. And remember, a lot of kids will now suffer less pain, have a better chance. We owe you and thank you.'

More applause. And Kim noticed that although Harry was clapping by her side, his face was set in the stony expression she had seen before.

She took a breath, hunched her shoulders. So far this evening she had done well. She'd see if her luck would run any further.

'I've seen happier faces than yours,' she said. 'I'm going home now. If you don't want to stay, you could claim that you have work to do and come back to my place for a coffee.'

'Coffee? No champagne, no sex like last time?'

'Neither champagne nor sex. Last time we had them was wonderful—but afterwards was more than I could take. But if you want coffee, it's on offer.'

She went to say goodbye to her new friends and then drove Bessie home. Once there she made sandwiches and put coffee on to percolate. If he came, fine. If he didn't, she could take the sandwiches to work. But somehow she knew he'd come.

He wasn't long, perhaps twenty minutes. She opened the door to him, silently motioned him to sit and poured him a coffee. Then she said, 'The extra five thousand pounds was your money again, wasn't it?'

'I told you before, it was never my money. It came to me by an accident of birth.'

'Just an accident? Did it come to you because you were next of kin or did she leave it to you in her will?'

He looked uncomfortable. 'She left it to me in her will.'

'So it was a deliberate act on her part. She wanted you to have the money. What did she die of?'

'Apparently she had a heart attack. It was very sudden, she certainly wasn't an old woman.'

'And you didn't go to the funeral?'

'I couldn't. It was over before I knew she was dead. But I didn't want to anyway.' He looked at her uncertainly. 'Why are you so interested, Kim?'

'Because I've had a rotten time recently. You've been avoiding me because you said you didn't want to get involved. Well, I think you picked on me because you didn't want to face up to things yourself.'

She saw anger flare in his eyes. He put down his cup with a crash and half rose to his feet. Then, very deliberately, he sat again. And to herself, she breathed a tiny sigh of relief.

'I've said it before—you don't care what you say, do you?'

'I care a lot. It scared me to say that. But I did it because I care for you.'

'I wonder if I really deserve you,' he muttered. 'But go on.'

'I think her leaving the money to you was a gesture, that she knew what she was doing. You've given fifteen thousand away—is there any left?'

'Quite a bit. I'll decide what charities to give it to.'

'I think you should spend it on yourself, as she wanted you to. If you could forgive her, it would make life easier for you.'

'Kim! I don't need to start having feelings for a woman who never had any for me!'

'She tried to make some amends. She was sorry! Now, give her credit for that and stop feeling so sorry for yourself!'

This time he did leap to his feet. His coffee spilled down him and his face was angrier than she had ever seen it.

'I'll fetch something to mop that up,' she said calmly.

For a moment they stared at each other. Then he said, 'It's OK. I'll just nip into your kitchen and use that paper roll. I was enjoying the coffee, too. Any chance of a refill?'

'No problem,' she said, and wondered if he could tell how her heart was thundering by the expression on her face.

When he returned he drank his coffee. Then he said, 'I feel as if I've been hit by a steam-roller. I hope you don't have this effect on your patients.'

'I just want you to be happy,' she said. She went to sit by him and kissed him. But it was a kiss of love, not passion, and the way he held her showed he wanted comfort more than anything.

Then he stood. 'I'd better go,' he said. 'I've got

things to think about. You're too good for me, Kim.
I wish I'd met you in a different life.'

'You can change, Harry, it's entirely up to you.
It'll hurt but it's not impossible.'

'Perhaps. But I'm happy the way I am.'

She thought for a moment. Things seemed to be
going her way tonight so she'd push her luck again.
'I've checked the rosters for next week,' she said.
'We've both got the same two days off. If you're not
doing anything…would you like to come to Cumbria
with me and stay the night with my parents?'

'What?'

'You've got this bad attitude to parents in general,'
she said. 'I love mine, always have done. I want you
to see what you can get out of having them, what
love there can be.'

'But if I go up there with you, they'll think that…'

'They'll think of you as a friend. And they live in
a lovely area, you can see the kind of life I'm going
to move into.'

'As a GP? I thought you might be thinking of
changing your mind.'

In fact, she *was* thinking of changing her mind.
But she was not going to tell him that. If he went to
Australia—then life as a GP would be great.

'So, are you coming home with me?' she asked.

Harry grinned and she knew that everything would
be all right. 'Yes, I'll come,' he said, 'if only because
you're the most unusual woman I've ever met. But
the minute your father asks me what my intentions
are, I'm off.'

'You'll have better things to talk about than intentions,' she said.

*   *   *

This had always been her home. Kim felt a surge of emotions as they dropped down the road to the small town on the edge of the Lake District where she had been born and brought up.

She pointed out places to Harry. 'That's where I used to wait for the school bus—the bus drivers used to hate the school run, we were always so noisy. And there's the stream I fell in when I was five. When I was younger I wasn't safe near any kind of running water. Oh, and, look, there's the Jester Café—it's been turned into a wine-bar! Harry, they can't do that!'

'Nothing stays the same,' he told her.

'But that's where I used to hang out with all my friends and plan my future. We could make a coffee last an hour and a half and the owner never minded. And look! There's the playing fields where I won the javelin event.'

It was only when they stopped at the traffic lights in the centre of the little town that she turned to look at Harry's face and caught the expression of sadness there. 'I'm sorry,' she said. 'I forgot, you never had a childhood like me, did you?'

'No. I had a good school, a couple of good teachers and I just worked like mad because I didn't have much social life. But I was happy. I had a plan.'

'You were happy?' she asked.

'No,' he said after a pause, 'I don't think I was. But I'm pleased that you had a childhood that you loved.'

Minutes later they pulled into the drive of Welleck House, her home. Her parents came out to meet them, and as always she hugged and kissed them. It was so good to see them! Then she turned to introduce Harry.

'This is Harry, my registrar. He's a friend and he's taught me so much.'

She caught a fleeting expression on Harry's normally bland face. An expression of longing? Who could tell? Well, if so, this was why she had brought him here. To see what he was missing, what family life could be like. Perhaps to see what he could have.

She had often brought friends—male and female—to visit her parents. But she watched with more care than usual to see how they reacted to Harry. 'Call us Martin and Joan,' her father said, shaking Harry's hand vigorously. 'We're very happy to meet you, Harry.'

'I'm really pleased to be here,' Harry said. 'I've heard so many good things about you.'

While Harry was busy talking to Martin, her mother looked at Kim, opening her eyes slightly in a silent question. Kim gave an equally slight shake of the head. No, she and Harry were not an item.

They went inside for a sandwich lunch—her parents never ate much in the middle of the day. 'So, tell me what you're learning,' her father asked her. 'Sounds interesting. I've never had an awful lot to do with prems, the hospital tends to take them.'

'We'll talk shop later, Dad. Right now I want to forget work. I want to sit here and gossip and enjoy myself.'

'You need to get out more,' Martin said. 'Fancy a trip on *Lake Lady*? I've booked her in case you do. Harry, do you sail?'

'Never have yet, but I'm willing to learn. What's the *Lake Lady*?'

Martin turned and pointed to a large photograph on the wall. 'That's her. A sailing boat, at least a hundred years old. A few of us found her lying derelict. We formed a consortium, bought her and paid a fortune to have her rebuilt. All in wood, of course. Now she's the most beautiful boat on Ullswater. It's old-fashioned sailing but it's fun.'

'Looks interesting. Now I know why Kim told me to pack my shorts.'

'I'll bet she told you to pack your boots as well.' Martin chuckled. 'Well, they'll do for tomorrow.'

After lunch they were all about to climb into Martin's battered Land Rover when his mobile phone rang. He looked at it suspiciously. 'I'm not supposed to be on call,' he said, 'but still… Hello. Julia… Yes, I know Marion Hebthwaite. I see… OK, I'll phone her then call in for five minutes. We're just on our way sailing. I'll let you know if there's any cause for anxiety but I doubt there will be. Right.'

He rang off, keyed in a number. 'Marion? Martin Hunter here. No, no, don't tell me over the phone, I'm coming over for a quick visit. But Julia, your health visitor is perfectly competent… Yes, I know she's young but she's not a child. I'm on my way.'

He rang off again and turned apologetically to Harry. 'That's the trouble when patients are friends as well. Marion Hebthwaite is now feeling guilty at asking me to come out. She knows she's being foolish but she can't help it. She's an older mother and she's just had her second baby.' Martin rubbed his hand over his eyes. 'The first one died after three months and this one isn't too strong. Now every little problem and Marion panics. And her husband is a soldier, away a lot.'

'I suppose her panic is understandable,' said Harry. 'Why isn't the baby too strong?'

Martin shrugged. 'Just the usual set of neonatal problems. She was born full term but very small. The hospital kept her in for a fortnight, just for observation. I've kept a close eye on her, thought she was making progress, but…we'll see.'

'May I come and have a look at her?'

Martin looked at him. 'A free consultation with a hospital paediatrician? Of course you can come and have a look.'

So they set off for a small house on the outskirts of the town and parked outside. Harry and Martin disappeared inside, Kim and her mother were left in the car to talk.

'I like him an awful lot better than Robin,' her mother said.

'So do I. But there's nothing in it, Ma. He's going to Australia soon, probably won't ever come back. He's just a friend.'

'Of course,' said her mother, obviously not believing a word of it. 'But, you know, he's very…fond of you. He looks at you when he thinks you won't notice, and his expression changes.'

'There's nothing in it,' Kim said firmly. 'Now, what's the news about this bypass for the town…?'

It was about fifteen minutes before Martin and Harry returned. Kim thought her father seemed abstracted, unusually thoughtful. 'Everything all right with the baby, Dad?' she asked.

Martin didn't answer at once. 'Either I learned something or perhaps two doctors are twice as good as one. I thought there'd be nothing seriously wrong. But Harry here suspects that there might be. We've phoned for an ambulance. Harry has talked to the paediatrician who'll be in charge and he'll do the necessary tests. You know, I'd have spotted that forty years ago.'

'Forty years ago it was a lot more common,' said Harry. 'Sadly, it's getting common again.'

'What are you both talking about?' asked Kim. 'I know you're supposed to maintain patient confidentiality—but I am a doctor.'

'I still may well be wrong,' said Harry. 'Only a chest X-ray and perhaps a culture will tell for sure. But I think the baby's got tuberculosis.'

'Tuberculosis?' said Kim, mystified. 'How could a baby catch tuberculosis up here?'

Harry shrugged. 'We talked to the mother. Apparently she and the baby spent a couple of weeks with her husband down near the London docks. These days, most people in this country with the disease catch it from those who bring it in from abroad. It's still not too common here but we're getting more and more cases.'

'And it's aerobic,' her father put in. 'Just a cough or a sneeze from an infected person can spread the disease.'

'Poor Mrs Hebthwaite,' said Kim. 'Have you told her what you think?'

'Certainly not,' said her father. 'We wait till the diagnosis is confirmed.'

Harry put in, 'There should be a happy outcome.

It's in the earliest stages and antibiotics should deal with it quite adequately.'

'I'm glad you came in with me,' Martin said.

'Now, she is beautiful,' Harry said reverently. 'You must spend all your time looking after her.'

'We all do our bit,' said Martin proudly. 'She's featured in half a dozen magazines. I'll show you the cuttings when we get home.'

They were looking at *Lake Lady*, a thirty-foot cutter, built of wood which was immaculately varnished. The trim was white, the fittings polished brass, the sails a dark red.

'She may look good but she's still a good sailor,' Martin went on. 'And if there's anything of a storm here, I'd rather be on board her than any of these modern boats.'

They climbed on board, hoisted the sails under Martin's directions, then cast off. There was only a light wind near shore, and at first they ghosted along gently. But when they caught the wind sweeping down from the peaks and along the valley, *Lake Lady* heeled and their speed increased. Kim smiled with the sheer exhilaration of it.

'So how d'you like sailing?' she called to Harry.

'I think this is just marvellous,' he said.

Of course, they were not as fast as the slender fibreglass boats around them, but it was *Lake Lady* that drew most of the admiring glances.

After a while Harry took the tiller and Martin coached him in how to respond to the wind, how to feel the boat. 'It's almost as if she were alive,' Harry said wonderingly. 'I've never tried anything like this.'

'I gather you're going to Australia,' Martin shouted at him. 'There's a lot of good sailing there.'

'I believe so. Now I've tried this, I think I'll get a boat of my own out there.'

'Start with a dinghy. Learn on something small—you'll be a better sailor with the bigger stuff.'

It was a good afternoon. They tacked to the far end of the lake, then anchored and had the picnic her mother had prepared. Then there was an exhilarating run back to the moorings. Yes, it was a good afternoon.

Kim was particularly interested to see how well Harry got on with her mother and father. And she knew he was quietly watching her, seeing how comfortable she was with her parents. There was nothing put on about it. This was how they had always been.

As soon as they got back to the house, Martin phoned the hospital and asked about Lucie Hebthwaite. Their provisional diagnosis had been confirmed. Lucie had tuberculosis. Her treatment had started and the doctors were very hopeful. 'Nice to get things right,' Kim's father said.

They had a late meal in the conservatory at home and sat around afterwards, talking about how medical training had altered in the past thirty years. The next day they went for a walk together and the weather remained good. 'It's not always like this,' Martin told Harry. And then they left—as arranged—quite early. They both had work the next day.

Her mother kissed Harry, her father shook his

hand and both said that they'd really like Harry to call again. And then it was back to Denham.

They drove back through the well-remembered places. Kim was silent, staring out of the window, recalling places, incidents, people she'd once known. Harry said nothing and she realised he had guessed what she was doing. But when they got onto the main road he asked, 'What is the biggest change between then and now?'

It was a good question, she thought about it. 'I still love the place but I suppose I'm a different person now,' she said. 'You know I've always intended to come back here, to work in Dad's place as a GP? Well…recently…I've been wondering. Home's still the same. But I feel that I'm changing.'

'It's good to be able to change.'

At first it sounded just like a casual remark. But there was something in the tone of his voice which made her wonder if there was some hidden message for her.

'So, did you enjoy yourself?' she asked. 'Going sailing and walking and so on?'

'You know I did. And we also know that that wasn't the reason that you took me. You took me to see your parents, to see what a happy family could be like. And I was both impressed and envious.'

'We're not all that unusual,' she pointed out. 'In fact, I think we're pretty ordinary.'

'Perhaps. But remember what your father said about Marion Hebthwaite when she phoned? She knew she was being foolish but she couldn't help it. Well, I know exactly how she feels. The joke is, of course, that she wasn't being foolish. But…I know exactly how she felt.'

Kim thought hard about what to say next. It was the first time Harry had ever accepted that he might be wrong, that there might be another way of behaving. 'I think you're big enough to be able to change your mind,' she said eventually.

'Perhaps. You're the only woman I've ever met who might persuade me that my attitude to life is wrong. But I just can't help it. I feel what I feel.'

'If you can't help yourself, no one can help you,' she said. 'And that, incidentally, is a very Harry Black remark.'

'You know me too well. Probably better than anyone.'

She decided not to say any more and for the rest of the journey they listened to music or chatted inconsequentially about work.

But she was thinking, debating with herself. She felt she had made progress with him, that they were closer than they had ever been. But she wanted to be closer still.

He drove her to her flat and she asked him in for coffee. And when they had finished, she took a deep breath. This was make-or-break time and she prayed that she was making the right choice.

'No strings, no promises, no conditions,' she said. 'I want you to stay the night. I want you to make love with me again.'

She saw his previously sleepy eyes come alert, flick towards her then take on that relaxed expression that, she knew, meant that he was thinking.

'And, please, please, don't make a joke of what

I've just said. It took a lot of effort and you're not to hide behind your sense of humour. You must be honest with me.'

His voice was hoarse. 'I'll try to be honest with you. I want to stay with you, I desperately want to stay with you. But I feel I shouldn't. It might make you…'

'Harry, I've half given you up,' she said. 'I know you're going to Australia, I just want to have some happiness before you go. It's not a lot to ask, is it?'

He came to sit beside her, kissed her. 'I want to so much,' he said, 'but…'

'Harry, I'm not a virgin. I've slept with you once already, lived with a man for three years. What I'm offering you I don't think is that important. We just want to—'

He grabbed her by the arms, shook her. 'Don't say that! It *is* important. What you are offering me is…is…' He seemed at a loss for words. 'It is important.'

He pulled her to her feet, wrapped his arms round her and kissed her, desperately. His lips were searing, demanding, forcing her to give that which she would have given willingly. She felt that she had never fully understood his hunger, his sheer need of her. And she knew that it was not just her body he desired, but her. Did he know that?

'It is important, to you and to me, isn't it?' he gasped. 'Isn't it important?'

'Yes, it's important,' she muttered. 'I don't know why I said that. But whatever I have to offer you, I want you to have it now.'

She remembered the last time they had made love.

It had been gentle, considerate, each trying to please the other, to find out what gave the other pleasure. But this time was different. She reacted to the need in him. They tore off each other's clothes and together they reached a frenzied climax minutes after they had tumbled onto the bed. Then they lay there, holding each other, both bathed in sweat.

'You give me so much,' he said. 'There is so little I can give you back. But lie there and I'll try.'

She watched curiously as he walked over to her chest of drawers and took out the candles. She had not used them since the last time they had been together in this bed. He lit them, turned to her. 'Now we start again,' he said. 'We'll lie here and be with each other and kiss each other. And if we want to go further than that, that's fine. If we don't want to go further, that's equally fine.'

So for an hour they lay in each other's arms. She thought she slept a little, but could feel his lips on her eyelids, the curl of her ears. Then, gently, they made love—she thought it a joining of two spirits, not two bodies, and it filled her with an indescribable joy. And then she slept.

Kim woke early, she had decided to. Carefully she slid out of bed. It was important that she didn't wake Harry. Then she turned to look at him. The sheet over his chest moved gently up and down. She could see his naked muscular shoulders, the strong column of his neck. When his eyes were closed his face looked younger, less watchful. The lines round his eyes disappeared, making him seem less alert, more contented. No time for thoughts like that now!

She had a sketchy wash, pulled on jeans and a T-shirt. Then she took two mugs of tea to the bedroom and shook him gently. 'Wake up, sleepyhead. The day's well started.'

'I was having a lovely dream, only it was true,' he mumbled. Then he sat up in bed, made a grab for her, which she evaded with ease.

'I liked it better when you were by my side when I woke up,' he told her. 'Getting up and dressed seems unfriendly.'

'I remember what happened the last time we woke up together,' she told him. 'There's no time for that now.'

'I think there is,' he said thoughtfully, 'or there could be.'

'Drink your tea, Harry. I need you awake. We need to talk and this is the only time.'

'Sounds serious. And I don't like serious talking. Remember, once you've said something it can be forgiven, but it can never be forgotten or unsaid.'

His words gave her strength. She was going to say something that she didn't want to be able to unsay. Even though she was already regretting starting. 'Come on, Harry, tea,' she said again.

He sat up, reached for the mug. The sheet dropped away from his shoulders, revealing his chest. Not thirty minutes ago she had been pressed to that chest and she felt that she could imagine its warmth still.

'If we have to talk, you could at least sit on the bed and let me hold your hand,' he said.

'Just my hand? Nothing else? Promise?'

'Promise,' he said.

So she sat by him on the bed, took his hand and

pressed it between her breasts. Then she laid it on her lap.

'I haven't known you very long,' she started, 'though it seems for ever. And every minute of our time together I can remember. I remember our first meeting, that weird feeling I had when I first saw you. After Robin I had intended to have a man-free six months. Get on with my work. But I saw you and my life was different. And you felt the same.'

'I did,' he admitted. 'It was strange.'

'Then we had a talk about what we were going to do, and we got involved in spite of ourselves. We talked about your daughter and we went to bed and made love and in general we just ambled through life, not getting anywhere. You told me that you distrusted other people and wouldn't commit yourself. I said you were wrong. And we kept seeing each other.'

'I did try not to hurt you,' he said hoarsely.

'You haven't hurt me. I've hurt myself. I've known what was happening and I've ignored it. My last hope was to take you to see my parents, to show you how people could live together and love and trust each other.'

She looked away from him, knew she couldn't face him when next she spoke. 'Last night was so marvellous that I felt I'd used up my ration of happiness. Perhaps I have. No matter, it was worth it. But it taught me one thing.'

'One thing?'

'I love you.'

She had said it. She didn't know whether the words would be a barrier between them or a gateway.

After a moment's silence she turned to look at him. His face was stricken. But he said nothing. And slowly, second by second, she felt her lonely chance of happiness slipping away.

'There's only one answer to that statement, Harry,' she said, 'and you missed it. You're meant to say that you love me, too. But you didn't, and I'm glad you've got the honesty not to pretend anything you don't feel. But now things have to end between us. We'll work together. You can teach me. And slowly I'll learn to be…be less fond of you.'

'Kim,' he said, 'I never wanted to—'

'It doesn't matter. Harry, you've never been anything less than honest with me and I wish you well. But you and me, as any kind of…partnership? We end now. I'm going for a walk down to town. You can let yourself out.'

Even at that moment she wondered. She left him time to call out, to say that they could talk about things, even to say that he loved her, too. But he didn't call. And so she slipped out of the door and set off across the grass, blinded with tears.

CHAPTER NINE

IN FACT Kim saw much less of Harry after that. The following weekend she was transferred out of SCBU and onto the normal neonatal ward. But before she went, Chris said, 'Remember, you've got an aptitude for this kind of work. You'd be a great SCBU doctor, Kim.'

'Possibly. But I think I'll be a GP,' she said.

She got a new set of people to work with, had to make new friends. This was ordinary, simple paediatric work, dealing with the newborn babies and their mothers, seeing that they were fine and sending them home as quickly as possible. She enjoyed it. This was the kind of work that she would do when she was a GP, this experience would be good for her.

She decided that the only way to get over Harry would be to immerse herself in work—and in play. So a typical day would begin with her doing a round of baby checks. Later on she would accompany the doctor in charge on the morning and afternoon rounds, dealing with possibly more serious conditions. And now she learned what to look for in the full-term, apparently healthy baby.

Much of the time she spent with Mark Forrest, who had been an SHO for four years now and was looking to become a specialist registrar. After a week in which she settled in, Mark took it on himself to teach her.

'Fifteen to twenty babies in a thousand suffer from an unstable hip,' he told her, 'so, of course, you check every baby. Don't ask me why, but more females suffer than males, and it's twice as likely to be the left hip as the right.'

They were looking down at a one-day-old baby, lying, apparently relaxed, on her back. Mark took one of the little girl's knees in each hand. 'See how I'm holding her,' he said to Kim, 'just with my fingertips but with the legs and hips at ninety degrees. Now, you hold her the same way.'

Gingerly, Kim did as she was told.

'Now, very very gently, press the hips back then lift the legs and move them outwards a little.'

Kim did as she was told, then gave a satisfied nod. 'I felt a tiny clunk in the left hip,' she said.

'Good. That's the head of the femur being lifted back into the socket. Now an unstable hip has been diagnosed, we can treat it. Catch it now and we can save an awful lot of trouble later.'

There were other things she learned that she knew would be useful to a GP, but she still missed SCBU.

In the evening she would swim or play badminton in the hospital gym. It filled her time and the weeks passed.

She was attractive, unattached, it was inevitable that she would be asked out. First of all she just declined with a smile, saying she was too busy, had too much to do. Then she accepted an invitation from Mark to go to the theatre and then to dinner.

It was a good play and the dinner was great. She had made an effort, spent time making herself up, dressing well. Mark was a pleasant companion, she quite enjoyed herself exchanging banter with him, swapping stories about awkward patients. And it was good to be out again, to feel that she was appreciated. But when Mark kissed her good night and asked if they could go out again, she said no.

'I've really enjoyed myself with you, Mark, but it would be unfair of me to lead you on. Sorry, I really am. But I'm carrying a torch for someone else.'

Mark laughed ruefully. 'Someone's a lucky chap,' he said. 'Good night, Kim.'

She just couldn't get over Harry. She saw him occasionally, they smiled at each other and passed the time of day. But she did the same with Chris or Erica. He was just an old friend.

But it hurt! Every time she saw him her heart thrashed in her breast, she felt herself colour, she knew if she wasn't careful she would stammer when she spoke to him. And the last thing she wanted was for him to feel sorry for her.

At first she had wondered, had hoped. He knew what she needed. If he wanted to, he could come to her, say that he would try. He would pull himself out from under the great weight of suspicion and anger that pinned him down. But he didn't come to her. He seemed to accept the situation. He was going to Australia. And Kim hid her misery by working.

She hadn't seen him for a week when they bumped into each other in the doctors' lounge in the main part of the hospital. Both were queuing for coffee and it would have looked strange to part at once. So they sat in adjoining leather armchairs and looked at each other warily.

'You might be interested,' she said. 'I phoned a

solicitor in Sheffield, told her about the equity and Robin and me. She leaned on Robin. I got a very good settlement, far more than I had expected. And I've had a letter from a friend to say that Robin has got another girl to move in with him. Apparently he needed help in keeping up the mortgage payments.'

'Hope she's got her name on the deeds,' said Harry.

There was an uneasy silence. Then she said, daringly, 'Will you tell me what you've done about your mother's personal stuff?'

After a moment's thought he took out his wallet, reached under the clear plastic window where so many people kept pictures. He offered her a little black and white photograph, much creased and worn. There was a small boy holding the hands of two smiling parents. 'Me aged four and a half,' he said. 'I was happy then. Apparently it was found in my mother's purse when she died. I've…looked through most of the other stuff.'

Kim drank her coffee quickly, gabbled something about work and then fled. Being with Harry was dangerous.

And then it was time to think about when her time at Denham would come to an end. She applied for a SHO posting in A and E at Sheffield. She was accepted.

'Harry's going soon,' Erica said.

Kim kept in touch with her old friends as much as possible, and was having lunch in the canteen with Erica. She was aware that her friend was watching her, assessing what effect her news would have.

'Well, we all knew he was going,' she said, trying to pretend that it meant little to her. 'Why so soon?'

'Apparently he's got a lot of holiday time owing. And we've appointed a replacement registrar. A Dr Marilyn King. Kim, she's terrible! She knows her stuff all right, but her attitude is that we're the nurses and she's the doctor, so she knows best. Of course, Chris has to support her, but we suspect that he's not too keen on her. And the gossip is that he's had words with her already. You know how keen he is on us working as a team.'

'I know,' said Kim.

'We get on so well with Harry,' Erica went on. 'Though even he's been…not quite himself recently. Not as sunny as he used to be.'

'Perhaps he's a bit worried about going to Australia,' Kim said.

'Perhaps.' Erica looked at Kim as if trying to make up her mind, then went on, 'You two had a row, didn't you? We all thought you were a perfect couple. And then suddenly it all fell apart. It was a pity. I don't suppose you could give him another chance? For all our sakes?'

'No,' said Kim. 'Some things are meant to work out, others are not. I liked Harry a lot. I still do but that's all.'

'Well, I tried,' said Erica. 'Now, what shall we have for pudding?'

And soon it was December, but there was no sign of any festive spirit. Denham was hit by a cold spell, and it snowed then snowed again. And to add to this misery there was a minor flu epidemic. Soon the hospital was trying desperately to cope with an increase in patients and a corresponding loss in staff.

Kim was asked if she'd mind moving back to SCBU for a while, she was needed there more than she was in the ordinary wards. Of course, she said yes. There was a bitter-sweet feel to the place. She had been so happy here. She was still happy in her work but every room brought back memories of Harry. And, of course, he was there. But he seemed to try as hard as possible to avoid her. Probably a good thing.

The weather got worse. Snow ploughs constantly moved up and down the main road, came into the hospital to clear a way for the ambulances to reach A and E. And the accident rate mounted. The orthopaedic wards filled with people who had slipped and broken limbs—especially elderly people.

Outside snow was heaped deep. When she walked back to her flat Kim was up to her knees or thighs in drifts. Well, she didn't mind the hard work. It took her mind off other things.

Then came the worst snowstorm of all. Denham was at a standstill. It was almost impossible to get in or out of the hospital. They were isolated. No matter, the hospital was warm, and if there was hardly anyone visiting the patients, it made things easier for the staff.

It was mid-evening, she was the only doctor in SCBU. Chris had phoned. He was stuck in Princess Mary hospital, would she mind covering for him? Harry was on duty at the main paediatric section, and if there was any big problem, she could bleep him.

'It's like the Western Front here,' she said, 'all

quiet. Not a parent in sight and no problems with any of the babies. It'll be an easy night.'

'When you think that, it's usually when you get into trouble,' Chris warned cheerfully. 'Harry's there if you need him.' And he rang off.

No, Kim thought to herself, Harry is not there when I need him.

The usual duties, observations, meticulous record-keeping. But it was a quiet night, and she found herself relying more and more on the coffee machine to keep herself awake. Then, at about ten, one of the trainee nurses came in and said, 'Kim, there was a man at the door. I've let him in. He seems pleasant enough. His name is Mr Landis, he says his baby was in here a few weeks ago. He says he's come to collect a few things that were left behind.'

'Thanks, Cath,' Kim said. 'But in future, when there's no receptionist on duty, ask a senior nurse before letting people in, won't you?'

Kim shivered. She remembered Mr Landis, the man whose baby died and who had maintained that completely emotionless expression all the way through. And yet everyone had known that he'd been suffering more than they could imagine. Kim had heard that his wife had been admitted to hospital, suffering from depression. Hadn't the family been through enough?

But what did he want now? When babies died on SCBU the parents often wanted some memento of their child—perhaps its wristband or something it had been wearing. Staff encouraged this. It enabled the grief-stricken parents to come to terms with their loss, helped them to closure. Some parents were photographed holding their dead child. But Kim thought Mr Landis had already collected what he wanted.

He had always been a courteous man, but Kim remembered talking to Harry about him—Harry had said never to trust a man who kept his emotions so much to himself. Now Kim was worried. She thought about bleeping Harry, then decided that she could deal with this herself.

Mr Landis hadn't changed at all, still the same wispy haircut, the same long mac. But now the mac was covered with melting snow. She found him in the second little nursery, talking to the one baby in there. He had lifted the lid of the incubator. 'Who's a lovely little Victoria? You've grown now, Victoria, so Daddy's going to take you to see Mummy. Mummy wants to see you and to hold you.'

And out of a bag he was carrying, Mr Landis took a large baby blanket.

Suddenly, Kim was terrified.

'Hello, Mr Landis,' she managed to say. 'I gather you want to see me?'

He turned, gave her a bland smile. 'Of course, Dr Hunter,' he said. 'Her mother and I just want to thank you for what you've done for little Victoria here. But now it's time to take her home.'

'That's not Victoria,' Kim said, dry-mouthed. 'That's Anna Stark and she can't be moved. She's not at all well and I'm going to put the incubator lid back on.'

She moved to where the incubator lid had been carefully placed. Mr Landis stepped in her way and frowned. 'This baby is Victoria Landis,' he said.

'Don't play games with me, Doctor. I'm taking her now. Her mother's coming home as well.'

'Mr Landis, your baby died! We don't want this one to die, too.'

Immediately she realised this had been exactly the wrong thing to say. She had angered the man. So she tried to back off, spoke in a conciliatory tone and said, 'Why don't you come to the doctors' room, have a coffee with me? Then we can talk about taking…Victoria to her mother.'

'Victoria is my baby. You can't stop me taking her!'

Kim thought of the snow outside and shivered. She walked round the man, got between him and the incubator and said, 'Mr Landis, I do think you—'

She should have guessed. Just for a moment she took her eyes off the man and glanced down at the baby. And the man hit her. Not too hard, but she was knocked flat and for a moment was sick and dazed. But now she was angry.

She rolled to her feet, staggered and saw that he had spread out the blanket, was reaching into the incubator. 'You're not taking that baby while she's in my charge!' She rushed across, body-charged him away from the incubator. 'Now get out of this ward!'

'She's my baby and I'm taking her! I knew you'd try to stop me so I came ready.' From the mac pocket he took a knife. She thought it was an old-fashioned carving knife, with a bone handle and a long, recently whetted blade. 'Now get out of my way!'

He moved towards her, waved the knife at her as if he was ready to use it.

'Mr Landis, why don't we sit down and…?' She

moved away from him until she backed into the incubator.

'Don't try and soft-talk me! Move away!'

'I won't!' she spat at him. 'Keep away from my baby!'

She grabbed for the blanket he had spread out, held it in her two hands. Somewhere she had read that a blanket or a cushion was a defence against a knife attack—at least it stopped you getting your hands cut. 'Mr Landis, you're in trouble, don't make things worse.'

He edged towards her, knife held ready.

She had another thought, a dim memory from a self-defence lecture. She screamed as loudly as possible. Mr Landis stopped, looked shocked. With her blanket-covered hands she grabbed for the knife, wrestled him away from the incubator and towards the door.

She was wild with rage and might have succeeded, but suddenly someone shouted 'Kim!' She turned her head to see Harry enter the room.

That moment of inattention was enough. There was a searing pain across her rib cage as the knife came free and sliced into her side. Then she fell. Her head smashed against the wall. As blackness took her, her last thought was for the baby she couldn't now protect.

She had a headache and a pain in her side. She didn't want to wake up but she had to. Her vision swimming, she opened her eyes. First she saw the IV line, dripping blood into her vein. And there was Harry, looking down at her. He was holding her hand.

'Harry?' she whispered.

He bent down to kiss her. 'You're all right now,' he said. 'You're in A and E. Everything is going to be fine.'

'The baby! What happened to the baby!'

'Anna slept peacefully through the entire performance and is still sleeping. But I checked her over just to make sure. She's fine—thanks to you. But if he'd taken her out into the cold...'

'And Mr Landis?'

'He's been sedated. He's sleeping with a policeman by his bedside.'

'Thank you, Dr Black, but it's my turn now for five minutes. You may stay if Dr Hunter wishes.'

A cheerful middle-aged face leaned over her, which Kim recognised as belonging to Peter Lord, the A and E consultant.

'Whatever you say, Peter,' Harry said. 'Kim, d'you want me to stay?'

Did she? 'Yes, I really do want you to stay,' she said.

Apparently her skull had been X-rayed while she'd been unconscious. After telling her this, Peter chatted to her for a while about nothing much in particular. She knew he was looking for signs of disorientation, which might suggest brain damage. But there were none. Finally he said, 'Can you remember what happened? Don't answer if it upsets you.'

'I remember the argument, the fight, everything until Harry came into the room. I'd have got that man out, but Harry distracted me.'

'Patient shows signs of annoyance at having lost a fight,' Peter said to Harry. Then he made the usual observations—checked pulse, BP, listened to her heart. He shone his torch in her eyes and muttered, 'Good. No sign of concussion so far. You've got a hard head, young lady. How's your side?'

'It hurts,' Kim said.

'Just a flesh wound. I've already sutured it. It'll hurt for a while and you certainly won't be back at work for a few days. But there should be no permanent damage.' Then his face went blank and he said, 'Another five inches to the left and that knife would have been through your heart. I don't know whether to compliment you on your bravery or tell you off for being foolish.'

'Don't do either. Just get me a cool drink.' Her mouth was drier than she could ever remember it.

'Fine. Now, we'll keep you in overnight, possibly longer. I'm going to give you a painkiller that will help you sleep. That side is going to hurt even more. And for five minutes only you can talk to Harry here. He's been a positive nuisance over the past couple of hours.' Peter fetched her a glass of water, and gave her a pill. Then he left.

Harry took her hand in both of his, kissed it. 'Do you know what I felt when I saw him stab you?' he asked.

That was a hard question. 'I don't want to think or talk,' she mumbled. 'I just want to be here and have you with me, holding my hand. I like it.'

'I like it, too. Kim, Peter was right. What you did was brave beyond belief. And if you can be brave like that, why can't I?'

But this question was too much for her. Her head

was swimming again and she knew she couldn't cope. 'I think I'll go to sleep now. You can go if you like.'

'I don't want to go,' he said. 'In fact, I won't.'

CHAPTER TEN

NEXT morning Kim was told that Harry had stayed with her for a further three hours, sitting there silently and holding her hand. Then he'd been bleeped because he'd been needed at SCBU and, of course, he'd gone at once. The young nurse who told her this thought that Harry was lovely. 'You're ever so lucky, having him,' she said.

'Anybody would be lucky, having him,' Kim said, and thought to herself, And that includes me.

The nurse helped her wash, fetched her a small breakfast and wrote up the obs. The IV line had been taken down, evidently she hadn't lost too much blood.

'Apparently you're a heroine,' the nurse went on. 'The whole hospital is talking about you. And there's been lots of enquiries about you.' She looked at Kim, wide-eyed. 'What's it like when someone comes at you with a knife?'

'It's not a lot of fun,' Kim said. 'If there are any more enquiries, just say I'm fine and I don't want any fuss.'

'Whatever you say,' said the nurse, obviously rather disappointed.

Just then a young female SHO came in, checked the nurse's obs and said she thought that Kim would be discharged later in the day. A nurse would call to see her regularly—it would be very handy since Kim lived in the hospital grounds.

'So can I go now?' Kim asked.

The SHO was horrified. 'You know better than that! The consultant wants a word first. Now, can I have a look at the sutures in your side?'

Peter Lord came a couple of hours later. He was amiable, reassuring and said that Kim could go home soon, he'd arrange an ambulance. 'You might have to talk to the police at some stage,' he said, 'but they say it can wait. That fellow Landis was sectioned this morning. There may well be no prosecution at all.'

Kim shivered. 'I don't want a prosecution,' she said. 'I can still feel sorry for him, poor devil, even though he did stab me.' Then she had to ask. 'Have you heard from Harry—Dr Black?'

Peter beamed at her. 'Sent word round,' he said. 'Apparently he's busy on the unit. The consultant hasn't returned yet and there's quite a backlog of work. But he'll come as soon as possible. The other good news is that the storm appears to be over and everything's starting to thaw. So we're going to get rid of you as we expect a great influx of patients.'

'I can go home!'

'You certainly can. But you can't go back to work. Now, you're a doctor, you know what I say is right. Don't try to be a heroine. Stay at home in bed, and you'll recover quicker.'

'Yes, doctor,' she said.

Shortly afterwards a wheelchair took her through A and E and an ambulance drove her the couple of hundred yards to her flat. She had found that she could walk—or hobble—and that she would be able to look after herself. But the district nurse would call.

So there she was in her bedroom in her flat. She appreciated being alone for a while. But she wondered where Harry was.

She had only a vague recollection of talking to him the night before, when she regained consciousness. He had said something about not going, about bravery. But what exactly she couldn't remember. Then she reminded herself that he would want to be with her anyway. She had been injured in his unit while he'd technically been in charge. He was a caring man, he'd want to be with anyone who had been injured who was working for him. Perhaps she was nothing special. But perhaps she was.

They'd hardly spoken over the past few weeks and when they had it had been as if they'd been strangers. She had told him that their affair was at an end. Why she should think that things would be different just because she'd been injured, she didn't know. But she did think things would be different. She wanted them to be different.

Put simply, she loved him.

At one o'clock there was a knock on her door. She had left it unlocked, the bedroom door open. 'Come in!' she called, thinking, hoping, knowing that it would be Harry. It wasn't. But it was almost as good—to her great surprise, there were her parents.

It was so good to see them. Her mother was in tears, her father speaking in that gruff way he had when he didn't want to reveal what he was feeling. They both kissed her—very carefully—then they sat by her bed to talk.

First, of course, she had to give her father a detailed medical account of her injuries and treatment. He seemed quite relieved, her mother wept more than ever.

'How did you get here?' Kim asked. 'How did you know?'

'Your friend Harry Black phoned early this morning. He told us what had happened, said you were in no danger and offered to pick us up off the train at York. It was good of him, we'd have been hours otherwise.'

Her mother lifted a plastic bag and said, 'Now I've seen that you're all right, I'm hungry and I'm thirsty. I'm going to make us all a cup of tea and a sandwich. Can you eat, Kim?'

'You bet,' said Kim. 'Kitchen is through there.'

Then, casually, she asked her father, 'So Harry called you?'

'Yes. He said he knew that we'd be the ones you'd want to see most. And he insisted that we stay at his flat for a couple of days—better than a hotel. He's going to come back in an hour or so and pick us up, suggested that we rest a while then come back to see you this evening. We're very grateful to him. He's quite a man, Kim.'

'I know,' Kim said. She was thinking that the apparently casual Harry was a demon at organising when he wanted to be. She wondered if he'd deliberately organised things so that he could have some time alone with her this afternoon.

And an hour later he did come. She was still tired, her side hurt. But when she saw him her heart gave that old familiar lurch and she knew that she loved him more than ever.

He looked concerned, leaned over to kiss her on the cheek. 'Sorry I've not been to see you earlier but I've been running round quite a lot and—'

'Harry, you've got my parents here and that's just about the best thing you could have done. You don't know how much I owe you.'

'You owe me nothing,' he said. 'Whatever I did, I did it because I wanted to.' Then he tried to revert to the old casual Harry. 'Look at these! The last cut flowers for sale in Denham. The lady who sold them to me said that after this it was plastic daffodils or nothing.'

He showed her a bunch of white orchids. 'Harry, they're lovely,' she said. And her mother said, 'I'll put them in a vase.'

'I've just phoned Peter Lord,' Harry went on. 'Most unprofessional of him, but he told me that you were in no great danger but that you should take it easy for a while. I've talked to Chris, he's organised a replacement for you and there'll be a small—or a large—deputation from the unit coming to see you this evening.'

'I'd better put on a fresh nightie,' she said. 'Now, apparently Ma and Dad are staying at your flat. There's only one bedroom—where are you going to sleep?'

He looked embarrassed. 'No problem. We expect to be busy on the unit—so for a day or two I've arranged to move into doctors' accommodation in the hospital.'

'Exactly where?'

'Well, as a matter of fact, in this block. I'll be able to bring you a cup of tea before leaving for work in the morning.'

She didn't dare look at her parents. But she could feel their amusement.

Soon after that all three left, saying that she needed to rest. Harry would take her parents to his flat and be back in an hour or so. He had to move in.

Kim stared at the ceiling and tried to think, tried to make sense of what was happening to her. Why was Harry doing so much for her? Then she decided that she just couldn't think. Perhaps it was the effect of the pain or the loss of blood or the drugs, but she couldn't think. Things would just have to happen to her. She closed her eyes and slept.

When she awoke she found him sitting by her bed-side. It seemed the obvious thing to reach out and take his hand. 'This is the second time in twenty-four hours that you've watched me wake up,' she said.

'I know. And it's where I want to be.' Then he said, 'Would you like a drink or anything?'

'More lemon barley water,' she said. She thought he seemed restless, not knowing what to say.

'It was good of you to send for my parents,' she said. 'How did you know that it was just the thing I'd want?'

'I think I know you now,' he said. 'I know what they mean to you, what they can do for you. I know…what I missed. And I now think it was partly my fault.'

'Your mother?' she asked.

'Well, perhaps she did cut me off. But then she

had no chance of making things better, did she?' He sighed. 'I'm glad you made me send for those personal effects. I looked through them again the other day and I found the draft of a letter. It was for me. It said how much she regretted what had happened but was there any chance of our meeting—just to see how things went?'

'And she died before she could send the letter?'

'She did. And now I feel sorry we didn't meet. But knowing that she wanted to come to see me…I feel more at peace with her. And at peace with myself.'

'I'm so glad, Harry,' she said.

He took her hand, kissed it again, then stood and walked over to the window. 'It's thawing faster than ever,' he said. 'Is there anything you want?'

'Yes, there is something I want. I want you to sit down, stop being so restless. And if there's anything you want to say, I want you to say it.'

So he sat. She took his hand squeezed it. 'I won't let you go,' she said.

He nodded. 'I've just had a word with Chris. Marilyn King, the woman who was taking my place as specialist registrar, has backed out. She didn't like Chris's style of medicine, said it wasn't disciplined enough. So she's going to a big London hospital instead. Chris asked if there was any chance of me staying on for a while—a month at the very least, but three or four months would be better.'

Kim felt her heart flutter, but she tried to keep calm. 'And you said?'

'Well, I phoned about the research place first. No problem. It doesn't matter when I start. Then I phoned the funding body. They didn't care when I started either. Any time over the next two years.' He paused. 'I got the feeling…that if I never went to Australia, the world of medicine would manage to survive somehow.'

Kim's mouth was dry, she reached for her barley water. 'It's nice to feel wanted,' she croaked. 'But what are you really saying?'

Again he pressed her hand to his lips.

'I'm making excuses again, aren't I?' he said. 'All my life I've made excuses for my behaviour. Now I'm going to stop.'

He squeezed his eyes shut and she stared at him, wondering, hoping.

'When I saw you facing that man, him holding a knife and you having only a tiny piece of cloth to defend yourself with…' He winced at the thought. 'I thought two things. First, if you had the bravery to risk your life, why didn't I have sufficient courage to risk—risk what? Getting hurt again? You have to trust someone some time, Kim. The other thing was—what would I do if you were dead? I realised at that moment that you were central to me. You fill my life and hopes and dreams. You're all I ever wanted, I just didn't have the sense to see it. I love you, Kim. Will you marry me?'

No need to think, she knew the answer at once. 'Of course I'll marry you. I've wanted to marry you since that first moment we met. So come and kiss me—carefully. Can we tell my parents?'

'Of course. And we can tell them how much I want them to be my parents, too,' he said.

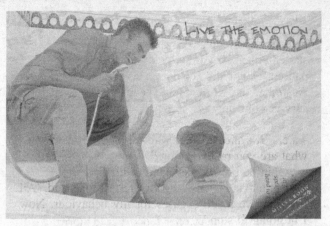

0804/03a

MILLS & BOON®

Live the emotion

Medical
romance™

THE BABY FROM NOWHERE *by Caroline Anderson*

Maisie McDowell watched her handsome new
neighbour's arrival with interest – but was horrified to
discover that James Sutherland was her new GP. Then
he told her she was pregnant – and she knew she
couldn't be. As the truth was gradually revealed James
was at Maisie's side to offer support...and more.

THE PREGNANT REGISTRAR *by Carol Marinelli*

(Practising and Pregnant)

When registrar Lydia Verhagh starts her new job on a
busy paediatric ward Dr Corey Hughes feels a natural
instinct to protect his pregnant colleague – and the
dramatic highs and lows of the special care baby unit
strengthen their bond. But does Corey truly appreciate
what it means to be a father to another man's child?

THE SURGEON'S MARRIAGE DEMAND
by Maggie Kingsley

(A&E Drama)

Consultant surgeon Seth Hardcastle was furious when
Dr Olivia Mackenzie got the A&E director's post. And it
got worse when he not only had to work with her –
but live with her too! They didn't agree on anything,
and he couldn't seem to charm her – yet he also
couldn't get her out of his mind!

On sale 3rd September 2004

*Available at most branches of WHSmith, Tesco, Martins, Borders,
Eason, Sainsbury's and all good paperback bookshops.*

MILLS & BOON

**Volume 3
on sale from
3rd September
2004**

Lynne
Graham

International Playboys

*The Desert
Bride*

*Available at most branches of WHSmith, Tesco, Martins, Borders,
Eason, Sainsbury's and all good paperback bookshops.*

FREE

4 BOOKS AND A SURPRISE GIFT!

We would like to take this opportunity to thank you for reading this Mills & Boon® book by offering you the chance to take FOUR more specially selected titles from the Medical Romance™ series absolutely FREE! We're also making this offer to introduce you to the benefits of the Reader Service™—

- ★ **FREE home delivery**
- ★ **FREE gifts and competitions**
- ★ **FREE monthly Newsletter**
- ★ **Books available before they're in the shops**
- ★ **Exclusive Reader Service offers**

Accepting these FREE books and gift places you under no obligation to buy; you may cancel at any time, even after receiving your free shipment. Simply complete your details below and return the entire page to the address below. You don't even need a stamp!

YES! Please send me 4 free Medical Romance books and a surprise gift. I understand that unless you hear from me, I will receive 6 superb new titles every month for just £2.69 each, postage and packing free. I am under no obligation to purchase any books and may cancel my subscription at any time. The free books and gift will be mine to keep in any case.

M4ZEE

Ms/Mrs/Miss/Mr......................................Initials ....
                                                                              BLOCK CAPITALS PLEASE

Surname ....

Address ....

....

....Postcode ....

Send this whole page to:
The Reader Service, FREEPOST CN81, Croydon, CR9 3WZ